TWO FOR THE HEART

TWO FOR THE HEART

THE PROPOSAL
by Betty Neels

THE ENGAGEMENT
by Ellen James

Chivers Press • G.K. Hall & Co.
Bath, Avon, England   Thorndike, Maine USA

This Large Print edition is published by Chivers Press, England, and by G.K. Hall & Co., USA.

Published in 1996 in the U.K. by arrangement with Harlequin Enterprises B.V.

Published in 1995 in the U.S. by arrangement with Harlequin Books S.A.

U.K. Hardcover ISBN 0–7451–2556–5 (Chivers Large Print)
U.K. Softcover ISBN 0–7451–2568–9 (Camden Large Print)
U.S. Softcover ISBN 0–7838–1213–2 (Nightingale Collection Edition)

The text of this Large Print edition is unabridged.
Other aspects of the book may vary from the original edition.

Set in 16 pt. New Times Roman.

Printed in Great Britain on acid-free paper.

British Library Cataloguing in Publication Data available

Library of Congress Cataloging-in-Publication Data

Two for the heart.
    p. cm.
    Contents: The proposal / by Betty Neels — The Engagement / by Ellen James.
    ISBN 0–7838–1213–2 (lg. print : lsc)
    1. Love stories.   2. Large type books.
I. Neels, Betty. Proposal.   II. James, Ellen. Engagement.
III. Title: Proposal.   IV. Title: Engagement.
[PR6064.E42P76 1995]
813′.08508—dc20
                                                    94–43668

THE PROPOSAL

CHAPTER ONE

The hazy early morning sun of September had very little warmth as yet, but it turned the trees and shrubs of the park to a tawny gold, encouraging the birds to sing too, so that even in the heart of London there was an illusion of the countryside.

The Green Park was almost empty so early in the day; indeed the only person visible was a girl, walking a Yorkshire terrier on a long lead. She was a tall girl with a tawny mane of hair and vivid blue eyes set in a pretty face, rather shabbily dressed; although her clothes were well cut they were not in the height of fashion.

She glanced at her watch; she had walked rather further than usual so Lady Mortimor, although she wouldn't be out of bed herself, would be sure to enquire of her maid if the early morning walk with Bobo had taken the exact time allowed for it. She could have walked for hours... She was on the point of turning on her heel when something large, heavy and furry cannoned into her from the back and she sat down suddenly and in a most unladylike fashion in a tangle of large dog, a hysterical Bobo and Bobo's lead. The dog put an enormous paw on her chest and grinned happily down at her before licking her cheek gently and then turning his attention to Bobo;

3

possibly out of friendliness he kept his paw on her chest, which made getting to her feet a bit of a problem.

A problem solved by the arrival of the dog's owner—it had to be its owner, she decided ... only a giant could control a beast of such size and this man, from her horizontal position, justified the thought; he was indeed large, dressed in trousers and a pullover and, even from upside-down, handsome. What was more, he was smiling...

He heaved her to her feet with one hand and began to dust her down. 'I do apologise,' he told her in a deep, rather slow voice. 'Brontes has a liking for very small dogs...'

The voice had been grave, but the smile tugging at the corners of his thin mouth annoyed her. 'If you aren't able to control your dog you should keep him on a lead,' she told him tartly, and then in sudden fright, 'where's Bobo? If he's lost, I'll never—'

'Keep calm,' begged the man in a soothing voice which set her teeth on edge, and whistled. His dog bounded out from the bushes near by and his master said, 'Fetch,' without raising his voice and the animal bounded off again to reappear again very shortly with Bobo's lead between his teeth and Bobo trotting obediently at the other end of it.

'Good dog,' said the man quietly. 'Well, we must be on our way. You are quite sure you are not hurt?' He added kindly, 'It is often hard to

4

tell when one is angry as well.'

'I am not angry, nor am I hurt. It was lucky for you that I wasn't an elderly dowager with a Peke.'

'Extremely lucky. Miss ...?' He smiled again, studying her still cross face from under heavy lids. 'Renier Pitt-Colwyn.' He offered a hand and engulfed hers in a firm grasp.

'Francesca Haley. I—I have to go.' Curiosity got the better of good sense. 'Your dog—that's a strange name?'

'He has one eye ...'

'Oh, one of the Cyclopes. Goodbye.'

'Goodbye, Miss Haley.' He stood watching her walking away towards the Piccadilly entrance to the park. She didn't look back, and presently she broke into an easy run and, when Bobo's little legs could no longer keep up, scooped him into her arms and ran harder as far as the gate. Here she put him down and walked briskly across the road into Berkeley Street, turned into one of the elegant, narrow side-streets and went down the area steps of one of the fine houses. One of Lady Mortimor's strict rules was that she and Bobo should use the tradesmen's entrance when going for their thrice-daily outings. The magnificent entrance hall was not to be sullied by dirty paws, or for that matter Francesca's dirty shoes.

The door opened onto a dark passage with white-washed walls and a worn lino on the

5

floor; it smelled of damp, raincoats, dog and a trace of cooked food, and after the freshness of the early morning air in the park it caused Francesca's nose to wrinkle. She opened one of the doors in the passage, hung up the lead, dried Bobo's paws and went through to the kitchen.

Lady Mortimor's breakfast tray was being prepared and her maid, Ethel, was standing by the table, squeezing orange juice. She was an angular woman with eyes set too close together in a mean face, and she glanced at the clock as Francesca went in, Bobo under one arm. Francesca, with a few minutes to spare, wished her good morning, adding cheerfully, 'Let Lady Mortimor know that Bobo has had a good run, will you, Ethel? I'm going over for my breakfast; I'll be back as usual.' She put the little dog down and the woman nodded surlily. Bobo always went to his mistress's room with her breakfast tray and that meant that Francesca had almost an hour to herself before she would begin her duties as secretary-companion to that lady. A title which hardly fitted the manifold odd jobs which filled her day.

She went back out of the side-door and round to the back of the house, past the elegant little garden to the gate which led to the mews behind the terrace of houses. Over the garage she had her rooms, rather grandly called by Lady Mortimor a flat, where she and her young

6

sister lived. The flat was the reason for her taking the job in the first place, and she was intent on keeping it, for it made a home for the pair of them and, although Lady Mortimor made it an excuse for paying her a very small salary, at least they had a roof over their heads.

Lucy was up and dressed and getting their breakfast. She was very like her sister, although her hair was carroty instead of tawny and her nose turned up. Later on, in a few years' time, she would be as pretty as Francesca, although at fourteen she anguished over her appearance, her ambition being to grow up as quickly as possible, marry a very rich man and live in great comfort with Francesca sharing her home. An arrangement, Francesca had pointed out, which might not suit her husband. 'I hate you working for that horrid old woman,' Lucy had said fiercely.

'Well, love,' Francesca had been matter-of-fact about it, 'it's a job and we have a home of sorts and you're being educated. Only a few more years and you will have finished school and embarked on a career which will astonish the world and I shall retire.'

Now she took off her cardigan and set about laying the table in the small sitting-room with its minute alcove which housed the cooking stove and the sink.

'I had an adventure,' she said to her sister, and over the boiled eggs told her about it.

'What kind of a dog?' Lucy wanted to know.

7

'Well, hard to tell—he looked like a very large St Bernard from the front, but he sort of tapered off towards the tail, and that was long enough for two dogs. He was very obedient.'

'Was the man nice to him?' asked Lucy anxiously, having a soft spot for animals; indeed, at that very moment there was a stray mother cat and kittens living clandestinely in a big box under the table.

'Yes—he didn't shout and the dog looked happy. It had one eye—I didn't have time to ask why. It had a funny name, too—Brontes—that's—'

'I know—one of the Cyclopes. Could you meet the man again and ask?'

Francesca thought about it. 'Well, no, not really...'

'Was he a nice man?'

'I suppose so.' She frowned. 'He thought it was funny, me falling over.'

'I expect it was,' said Lucy. 'I'd better go or I'll miss the bus.'

After Lucy had gone she cleared away the breakfast things, tidied the room and their bedroom, and made sure that she herself was tidy too, and then she went back to the house. She was expected to lunch off a tray at midday and she seldom got back until six o'clock each evening; she arranged food for the cat, made sure that the kittens were alive and well, and locked the door.

Her employer was still in bed, sitting up

against lacy pillows, reading her letters. In her youth Lady Mortimor had been a handsome woman; now in her fifties, she spent a good part of her days struggling to retain her looks. A facelift had helped; so had the expert services of one of the best hairdressers in London and the daily massage sessions and the strict diet, but they couldn't erase the lines of discontent and petulance.

Francesca said good morning and stood listening to the woman's high-pitched voice complaining of lack of sleep, the incompetence of servants and the tiresome bills which had come in the post. When she had finished Francesca said, as she nearly always did, 'Shall I attend to the bills first, Lady Mortimor, and write the cheques and leave them for you to sign? Are there any invitations you wish me to reply to?'

Lady Mortimor tossed the pile of letters at her. 'Oh, take the lot and endeavour to deal with them—is there anything that I should know about this morning?'

'The household wages,' began Francesca, and flushed at Lady Mortimor's snide,

'Oh, to be sure you won't forget those...'

'Dr Kennedy is coming to see you at eleven o'clock. Will you see him in the morning-room?'

'Yes, I suppose so; he really must do something about my palpitations—what else?'

'A fitting for two evening gowns at Estelle,

9

lunch with Mrs Felliton.'

'While I am lunching you can get my social diary up to date, do the flowers for the dining-room, and go along to the dry-cleaners for my suit. There will be some letters to type before you go, so don't idle away your time. Now send Ethel to me, have the cheques and wages book ready for me by half-past ten in the morning-room.' As Francesca went to the door she added, 'And don't forget little Bobo...'

'Thank you or please would be nice to hear from time to time,' muttered Francesca as she went to get the wages book, a weekly task which at least gave her the satisfaction of paying herself as well as the rest of the staff. She entered the amounts, got out the cash box from the wall safe and put it ready for Lady Mortimor, who liked to play Lady Bountiful on Fridays and pay everyone in cash. The bills took longer; she hadn't quite finished them when Maisie, the housemaid, brought her a cup of coffee. She got on well with the staff— with the exception of Ethel, of course; once they saw that she had no intention of encroaching on their ground, and was a lady to boot, with a quiet voice and manner, they accepted her for what she was.

Lady Mortimor came presently, signed the cheques, handed out the wages with the graciousness of royalty bestowing a favour and, fortified with a tray of coffee, received Dr Kennedy, which left Francesca free to tidy the muddled desk she had left behind her and take Bobo for his midday walk, a brisk twenty minutes or so before she went back to eat her lunch off a tray in the now deserted morning-room. Since the lady of the house was absent, Cook sent up what Maisie described as a nice little bit of hake with parsley sauce, and a good, wholesome baked custard to follow.

Francesca ate the lot, drank the strong tea which went with it and got ready to go to the cleaners. It wasn't far; Lady Mortimor patronised a small shop in Old Bond Street and the walk was a pleasant one. The day had turned out fine as the early morning had indicated it might and she allowed her thoughts to roam, remembering wistfully the pleasant house in Hampstead Village where they had lived when her parents had been alive. That had been four years ago now; she winced at the memory of discovering that the house had been mortgaged and the debts so large that they had swallowed up almost all the money there was. The only consolation had been the trust set aside for Lucy's education so that she had been able to stay on as a day pupil at the same well-known school.

There had been other jobs of course, after learning typing and shorthand at night-school while they lived precariously with her mother's elderly housekeeper, but she had known that she would have to find a home of their own as quickly as possible. Two years ago she had answered Lady Mortimor's advertisement and since it offered a roof over their heads and there was no objection to Lucy, provided she never entered the house, she had accepted it, aware that her wages were rather less than Maisie's and knowing that she could never ask for a rise: Lady Mortimor would point out her free rooms and all the advantages of working in a well-run household and the pleasant work.

All of which sounded all right but in practice added up to ten hours a day of taking orders with Sundays free. Well, she was going to stay until Lucy had finished school—another four years. I'll be almost thirty, thought Francesca gloomily, hurrying back with the suit; there were still the flowers to arrange and the diary to bring up to date, not to mention the letters and a last walk for Bobo.

It was pouring with rain the next morning, but that didn't stop Bobo, in a scarlet plastic coat, and Francesca, in a well-worn Burberry, now in its tenth year, going for their morning walk. With a scarf tied over her head, she left Lucy getting dressed, and led the reluctant little dog across Piccadilly and into the Green Park. Being Saturday morning, there were very few people about, only milkmen and postmen and some over-enthusiastic joggers. She always went the same way for if by any evil chance Bobo should run away and get lost, he had more chance of staying around a part of the park with which he was familiar. The park was even emptier than the streets and, even if Francesca had allowed herself to hope that she might meet the man and his great dog, common sense told her that no one in their right mind would do more than give a dog a quick walk through neighbouring streets.

They were halfway across the park, on the point of turning back, when she heard the beast's joyful barking and a moment later he came bounding up. She had prudently planted her feet firmly this time but he stopped beside her, wagging his long tail and gently nuzzling Bobo before butting her sleeve with his wet head, his one eye gleaming with friendliness.

His master's good-morning was genial. 'Oh, hello,' said Francesca. 'I didn't expect you to be here—the weather's so awful.'

A remark she instantly wished unsaid; it sounded as though she had hoped to meet him. She went pink and looked away from him and didn't see his smile.

'Ah—but we are devoted dog owners, are we not?' he asked easily. 'And this is a good place for them to run freely.'

'I don't own Bobo,' said Francesca, at pains not to mislead him. 'He belongs to Lady Mortimor; I'm her companion.'

He said, half laughing, 'You don't look in the least like a companion; are they not ladies who find library books and knitting and read aloud? Surely a dying race.'

If he only knew, she thought, but all she said

cheerfully was, 'Oh, it's not as bad as all that, and I like walking here with Bobo. I must go.'

She smiled at him from her pretty, sopping-wet face. 'Goodbye, Mr Pitt-Colwyn.'

'*Tot ziens*, Miss Francesca Haley.'

She bent to pat Brontes. 'I wonder why he has only one eye?' she said to herself more than to him, and then walked briskly away, with Bobo walking backwards in an effort to return to his friend. Hurrying now, because she would be late back, she wondered what he had said instead of goodbye—something foreign and, now she came to think of it, he had a funny name too; it had sounded like Rainer, but she wasn't sure any more.

It took her quite a while to dry Bobo when they got back, and Ethel, on the point of carrying Lady Mortimor's tray upstairs, looked at the kitchen clock in triumph.

Francesca saw the look. 'Tell Lady Mortimor that I'm late back, by all means,' she said in a cool voice. 'You can tell her too that we stayed out for exactly the right time but, unless she wishes Bobo to spoil everything in her bedroom, he needs to be thoroughly dried. It is raining hard.'

Ethel sent her a look of dislike and Cook, watching from her stove, said comfortably, 'There's a nice hot cup of tea for you, Miss Haley; you drink it up before you go to your breakfast. I'm sure none of us wants to go out in such weather.'

14

Ethel flounced away, Bobo at her heels, and Francesca drank her tea while Cook repeated all the more lurid news from the more sensational Press. 'Don't you take any notice of that Ethel, likes upsetting people, she does.'

Francesca finished her tea. 'Well, she doesn't need to think she'll bother me, Cook, and thanks for the tea, it was lovely.'

Lucy would be home at midday since it was Saturday, and they made the shopping list together since she was the one who had to do it.

'Did you see him again?' asked Lucy.

'Who?' Francesca was counting out the housekeeping money. 'The man and his great dog? Yes, but just to say good morning.' She glanced up at her sister. 'Do you suppose I should go another way round the park? I mean, it might look as though I was wanting to meet him.'

'Well don't you?'

'He laughs at me—oh, not out loud, but behind his face.'

'I shall come with you tomorrow and see him for myself.'

On Sundays Francesca took Bobo for his morning run before being allowed the rest of the day free. 'He's not likely to be there so early on a Sunday...'

'All the same, I'll come. What shall we do tomorrow? Could we go to Regent Street and look at the shops? And have something at McDonald's?'

'All right, love. You need a winter coat...'

'So do you. Perhaps we'll find a diamond ring or a string of pearls and get a reward.'

Francesca laughed. 'The moon could turn to cheese. My coat is good for another winter— I've stopped growing but you haven't. We'll have a good look around and when I've saved enough we'll buy you a coat.'

Lady Mortimor had friends to lunch which meant that Francesca had to do the flowers again and then hover discreetly in case her employer needed anything.

'You may pour the drinks,' said Lady Mortimor graciously, when the guests had settled themselves in the drawing-room, and then in a sharp aside, 'and make sure that everyone gets what she wants.'

So Francesca went to and fro with sherry and gin and tonic and, for two of the ladies, whisky. Cool and polite, aware of being watched by critical eyes, and disliking Lady Mortimor very much for making her do something which Crow the butler should be doing. Her employer had insisted that when she had guests for lunch it should be Francesca who saw to the drinks; it was one of the spiteful gestures she made from time to time in order, Francesca guessed, to keep her in her place. Fortunately Crow was nice about it; he had a poor opinion of his mistress, the widow of a wholesale textile manufacturer who had given away enough money to be knighted, and he

16

knew a lady born and bred when he saw Francesca, as he informed Cook.

When the guests had gone, Lady Mortimor went out herself. 'Be sure and have those letters ready for me—I shall be back in time to dress,' she told Francesca. 'And be sure and make a note in the diary—Dr Kennedy is bringing a specialist to see me on Tuesday morning at ten o'clock. You will stay with me of course—I shall probably feel poorly.'

Francesca thought that would be very likely. Eating too much rich food and drinking a little too much as well ... She hoped the specialist would prescribe a strict diet, although on second thoughts that might not do—Lady Mortimor's uncertain temper might become even more uncertain.

Sundays were wonderful days; once Bobo had been taken for his walk she was free, and even the walk was fun for Lucy went with her and they could talk. The little dog handed over to a grumpy Ethel, they had their breakfast and went out, to spend the rest of the morning and a good deal of the afternoon looking at the shops, choosing what they would buy if they had the money, eating sparingly at McDonald's and walking back in the late afternoon to tea in the little sitting-room and an evening by the gas fire with the cat and kittens in their box between them.

Monday always came too soon and this time there was no Brontes to be seen, although the morning was fine. Francesca went back to the house to find Lady Mortimor in a bad temper so that by the end of the day she wanted above all things to rush out of the house and never go back again. Her ears rang with her employer's orders for the next day. She was to be earlier than usual—if Lady Mortimor was to be ready to be seen by the specialist then she would need to get up earlier than usual, which meant that the entire household would have to get up earlier too. Francesca, getting sleepily from her bed, wished the man to Jericho.

Lady Mortimor set the scene with all the expertise of a stage manager; she had been dressed in a velvet housecoat over gossamer undies, Ethel had arranged her hair in artless curls and tied a ribbon in them, and she had made up carefully with a pale foundation. She had decided against being examined in her bedroom; the *chaise-longue* in the dressing-room adjoining would be both appropriate and convenient. By half-past nine she was lying, swathed in shawls, in an attitude of resigned long-suffering.

There was no question of morning coffee, of course, and that meant that Francesca didn't get any either. She was kept busy fetching the aids Lady Mortimor considered vital to an invalid's comfort: eau-de-Cologne, smelling salts, a glass of water...

'Mind you pay attention,' said that lady. 'I shall need assistance from time to time and probably the specialist will require things held or fetched.'

Francesca occupied herself wondering what these things might be. Lady Mortimor kept talking about a specialist, but a specialist in what? She ventured to ask and had her head bitten off with, 'A heart consultant of course, who else? The best there is—I've never been one to grudge the best in illness...'

Francesca remembered Maisie and her scalded hand a few months previously. Lady Mortimor had dismissed the affair with a wave of the hand and told her to go to Out-patients during the hour she had off each afternoon. Her tongue, itching to give voice to her strong feelings, had to be held firmly between her teeth.

Ten o'clock came, with no sign of Dr Kennedy and his renowned colleague, and Lady Mortimor, rearranging herself once again, gave vent to a vexed tirade. 'And you, you stupid girl, might have had the sense to check with the consulting-rooms to make sure that this man has the time right. Really, you are completely useless...'

Francesca didn't say a word; she had lost her breath for the moment, for the door had opened and Dr Kennedy followed by Mr Pitt-Colwyn were standing there. They would have heard Lady Mortimor, she thought miserably, and would have labelled her as a useless female at everyone's beck and call.

'Well, can't you say something?' asked Lady Mortimor and at the same time became aware of the two men coming towards her, so that her cross face became all charm and smiles and her sharp voice softened to a gentle, 'Dr Kennedy, how good of you to come. Francesca, my dear, do go and see if Crow is bringing the coffee—'

'No coffee, thank you,' said Dr Kennedy. 'Here is Professor Pitt-Colwyn, Lady Mortimor. You insisted on the best heart specialist, and I have brought him to see you.'

Lady Mortimor put out a languid hand. 'Professor—how very kind of you to spare the time to see me. I'm sure you must be a very busy man.'

He hadn't looked at Francesca; now he said with grave courtesy, 'Yes, I am a busy man, Lady Mortimor.' He pulled up a chair and sat down. 'If you will tell me what is the trouble?'

'Oh, dear, it is so hard to begin—I have suffered poor health every day since my dear husband died. It is hard to be left alone at my age—with so much life ahead of me.' She waved a weak hand. 'I suffer from palpitations, Professor, really alarmingly so; I am convinced that I have a weak heart. Dr Kennedy assures me that I am mistaken, but you know what family doctors are, only too anxious to reassure one if one is suffering from some serious condition...'

Professor Pitt-Colwyn hadn't spoken, there was no expression upon his handsome face and

20

Francesca, watching from her discreet corner, thought that he had no intention of speaking, not at the moment at any rate. He allowed his patient to ramble on in a faint voice, still saying nothing when she paused to say in a quite different tone, 'Get me some water, Francesca, can't you see that I am feeling faint? And hurry up, girl.'

The glass of water was within inches of her hand. Francesca handed it, quelling a powerful desire to pour its contents all over Lady Mortimor's massive bosom.

She went back to her corner from where she admired the professor's beautiful tailored dark grey suit. He had a nice head too, excellent hair—she considered the sprinkling of grey in it was distinguished—and he had nice hands. She became lost in her thoughts until her employer's voice, raised in barely suppressed temper, brought her back to her surroundings.

'My smelling salts—I pay you to look after me, not stand there daydreaming—' She remembered suddenly that she had an audience and added in a quite different voice, 'Do forgive me—I become so upset when I have one of these turns, I hardly know what I'm saying.'

Neither man answered. Francesca administered the smelling salts and the professor got to his feet. 'I will take a look at your chest, Lady Mortimor,' and he stood aside while Francesca removed the shawls and the housecoat and laid a small rug discreetly over the patient's person.

The professor had drawn up a chair, adjusted his stethoscope and begun his examination. He was very thorough and when he had done what was necessary he took her blood-pressure, sat with Lady Mortimor's hand in his, his fingers on her pulse.

Finally he asked, 'What is your weight?'

Lady Mortimor's pale make-up turned pink. 'Well, really I'm not sure ...' She looked at Francesca, who said nothing, although she could have pointed out that within the last few months a great many garments had been let out at the seams ...

'You are overweight,' said the professor in measured tones, 'and that is the sole cause of your palpitations. You should lose at least two stone within the next six months, take plenty of exercise—regular walking is to be recommended—and small light meals and only moderate drinking. You will feel and look a different woman within that time, Lady Mortimor.'

'But my heart—'

'It is as sound as a bell; I can assure you that there is nothing wrong with you other than being overweight.'

He got up and shook her hand. 'If I may have a word with Dr Kennedy—perhaps this young lady can show us somewhere we can be private.'

22

'You are hiding something from me,' declared Lady Mortimor. 'I am convinced that you are not telling me the whole truth.'

His eyes were cold. 'I am not in the habit of lying, Lady Mortimor; I merely wish to discuss your diet with Dr Kennedy.'

Francesca had the door open and he went past her, followed by Dr Kennedy. 'The morning-room,' she told them. 'There won't be anyone there at this time in the morning.'

She led the way and ushered them inside. 'Would you like coffee?'

The professor glanced at his companion and politely declined, with a courteous uninterest which made her wonder if she had dreamed their meetings in the park. There was no reason why he shouldn't have made some acknowledgement of them—not in front of Lady Mortimor, of course. Perhaps now he had seen her here he had no further interest; he was, she gathered, an important man in his own sphere.

She went back to Lady Mortimor and endured that lady's peevish ill humour for the rest of the day. The next day would be even worse, for by then Dr Kennedy would have worked out a diet.

Of course, she told Lucy when at last she was free to go to her rooms.

'I say, what fun—was he pompous?'

'No, not in the least; you couldn't tell what he was thinking.'

'Oh, well, doctors are always poker-faced. He might have said hello.'

Francesca said crossly, 'Why should he? We haven't anything in common.' She added a little sadly, 'Only I thought he was rather nice.'

Lucy hugged her. 'Never mind, Fran, I'll find you a rich millionaire who'll adore you forever and you'll marry him and live happily ever after.'

Francesca laughed. 'Oh, what rubbish. Let's get the washing-up done.'

As she set out with Bobo the next morning, she wished that she could have taken a different route and gone at a different time, but Lady Mortimor, easy-going when it came to her own activities and indifferent as to whether they disrupted her household, prided herself on discipline among her staff; she explained this to her circle of friends as caring for their welfare, but what it actually meant was that they lived by a strict timetable and since, with the exception of Francesca, she paid them well and Cook saw to it that the food in the kitchen was good and plentiful, they abided by it. It was irksome to Francesca and she was aware that Lady Mortimor knew that; she also knew that she and Lucy needed a home and that not many people were prepared to offer one.

So Francesca wasn't surprised to see Brontes bounding to meet her, followed in a leisurely manner by his master. She was prepared for it, of course; as he drew level she wished him a cold good-morning and went on walking, towing Bobo and rather hampered by Brontes bouncing to and fro, intent on being friendly.

Professor Pitt-Colywn kept pace with her. 'Before you go off in high dudgeon, be good enough to listen to me.' He sounded courteous; he also sounded as though he was in the habit of being listened to if he wished.

'Why?' asked Francesca.

'Don't be silly. You're bristling with indignation because I ignored you yesterday. Understandable, but typical of the female mind. No logic. Supposing I had come into the room exclaiming, "Ah, Miss Francesca Haley, how delightful to meet you again"—and it was delightful, of course—how would your employer have reacted?' He glanced at her thoughtful face. 'Yes, exactly, I have no need to dot the *I*s or cross the *T*s. Now that that slight misunderstanding is cleared up, tell me why you work for such a tiresome woman.'

She stood still the better to look at him. 'It is really none of your business...'

He brushed that aside. 'That is definitely something I will decide for myself.' He smiled down at her. 'I'm a complete stranger to you; you can say anything you like to me and I'll forget it at once if you wish me to—'

'Oh, the Hippocratic oath.'

His rather stern mouth twitched. 'And that too. You're not happy there, are you?'

She shook her head. 'No, and it's very kind

25

of you to—to bother, but there is really nothing to be done about it.'

'No, there isn't if you refuse to tell me what is wrong.' He glanced at his watch. 'How long do you have before you have to report back?'

'Fifteen minutes.'

'A lot can be said in that time. Brontes and I will walk back with you as far as Piccadilly.'

'Oh, will you?'

'Did I not say so?' He turned her round smartly, and whistled to Brontes. 'Now consider me your favourite uncle,' he invited.

CHAPTER TWO

Afterwards Francesca wondered what had possessed her. She had told Professor Pitt-Colwyn everything. She hadn't meant to, but once she got started she had seemed unable to stop. She blushed with shame just remembering it; he must have thought her a complete fool, sorry for herself, moaning on and on about her life. That this was a gross exaggeration had nothing to do with it; she would never be able to look him in the face again. The awful thing was that she would have to unless he had the decency to walk his dog in another part of the park.

She was barely in the park before he joined her.

'A splendid morning,' he said cheerfully. 'I enjoy the autumn, don't you?' He took Bobo's lead from her and unclipped it. 'Let the poor, pampered beast run free. Brontes will look after him; he has a strong paternal instinct.'

It was difficult to be stand-offish with him. 'He's a nice dog, only he's—he's rather a mixture, isn't he?'

'Oh, decidedly so. Heaven knows where he got that tail.'

For something to say, for she was feeling suddenly shy, 'He must have been a delightful puppy.'

'I found him in a small town in Greece. Someone had poked out his eye and beaten him almost to death—he was about eight weeks old.'

'Oh, the poor little beast—how old is he now?'

'Eight months old and still growing. He's a splendid fellow and strangely enough, considering his origin, very obedient.'

'I must get back.' She looked around for Bobo, who was nowhere in sight, but in answer to her companion's whistle Brontes came trotting up with Bobo scampering beside him. The professor fastened his lead and handed it to her. His goodbye was casually kind; never once, she reflected as she walked back to the house, had he uttered a word about her beastly job. She had been a great fool to blurt out all her worries and grumbles to a complete

27

stranger who had no interest in her anyway. She wished most heartily that there was some way in which she could avoid meeting him ever again.

She thought up several schemes during the course of the day, none of which held water, and which caused her to get absent-minded so that Lady Mortimor had the pleasure of finding fault with her, insisting that she re-type several letters because the commas were in the wrong place. It was after seven o'clock by the time Francesca got back to her room over the garage and found Lucy at her homework.

'You've had a beastly day.' Lucy slammed her books shut and got out a cloth and cutlery. 'I put some potatoes in the oven to bake; they'll be ready by now. We can open a tin of beans, too. The kettle's boiling; I'll make a cup of tea.'

'Lovely, darling, I've had a tiresome day. How's school? Did you get an A for your essay?'

'Yes. Did you see him this morning?'

'Yes, just for a moment...'

'Didn't you talk at all?'

'Only about his dog.' Francesca poured them each a cup of tea and then sat down to drink it. 'I wish I'd never told him—'

'Oh, pooh—I dare say he's forgotten already. He must have lots of patients to think about; his head must be full of people's life histories.'

Francesca opened the tin of beans. 'Yes, of

course, only I wish I need never see him again.'

To her secret unacknowledged chagrin, it seemed that she was to have her wish. He wasn't there the following morning, nor for the rest of the week; she told herself that it was a great relief and said so to Lucy, who said, 'Rubbish, you know you want to see him again.'

'Well—yes, perhaps. It was nice to have someone to talk to.' Francesca went on briskly, 'I wonder if it would be a good idea to go to evening classes when they start next month?'

Lucy looked at her in horror. 'Darling, you must be crazy—you mean sit for two hours learning Spanish or how to upholster a chair? I won't let you. Don't you see the kind of people who go to evening classes are very likely like us—without friends and family? Even if you got to know any of them they'd probably moan about being lonely...'

Francesca laughed. 'You know that's not quite true,' she said, 'although I do see what you mean.'

'Good. No evening classes. Doesn't Lady Mortimor have men visitors? She's always giving dinner parties...'

Francesca mentally reviewed her employer's guests; they were all past their prime. Well-to-do, self-satisfied and loud-voiced. They either ignored her in the same way as they ignored Crow or Maisie, or they made vapid remarks like, 'How are you today, little girl?'

Which, since she was all of five feet ten inches tall and splendidly built, was an extremely silly thing to say.

She said, laughing, 'I can't say I've ever fancied any of them. I shall wait until you are old enough and quite grown-up, and when you've found yourself a millionaire I shall bask in your reflected glory.' She began to clear the table. 'Let's get Mum fed while the kittens are asleep—and that's another problem ....'

September remained fine until the end of the month, when wind and rain tore away the last vestiges of summer. Francesca and Bobo tramped their allotted routine each morning and returned, Bobo to be fussed over once he had been dried and brushed, Francesca to hurry to her rooms, gobble breakfast and dash back again to start on the hundred and one jobs Lady Mortimor found for her to do, which were never done to that lady's satisfaction. The strict diet to which Professor Pitt-Colwyn had restricted her might be reducing her weight, but it had increased her ill humour. Francesca, supervising the making of a salad-dressing with lemon juice to accompany the thin slices of chicken which constituted her employer's lunch, wished that he had left well alone. Let the woman be as fat as butter if she wished, she reflected savagely, chopping a head of chicory while she listened to Cook detailing the menu for the dinner party that evening. A pity the professor couldn't hear that; it was dripping with calories...

Because of the dinner party the staff lunch was cold meat and potatoes in their jackets and Francesca, knowing the extra work involved in one of Lady Mortimor's large dinner parties, had hers in the kitchen and gave a hand with the preparations.

All the guests had arrived by the time she left the house that evening; Lady Mortimor, overpoweringly regal in purple velvet, had made her rearrange the flowers in the hall, polish the glasses again, much to Maisie's rage, and then go to the kitchen to make sure that Cook had remembered how to make sweet and sour sauce, which annoyed the talented woman so much that she threatened to curdle it.

'A good thing it's Sunday tomorrow,' said Francesca, eating toasted cheese while Lucy did her homework. 'And I must think of something for the kittens.' They peered at her, snug against their mother in the cardboard box, and the very idea of finding happy homes for them worried her. How was she to know if the homes were happy and what their mother would do without them?

They went to bed presently, and she dreamt of kittens and curdled sauce and Lady Mortimor in her purple, to wake unrefreshed. At least it wasn't raining, and Lucy would go with her and Bobo, and after breakfast they would go and look at the shops, have a snack

31

somewhere and go to evensong at St Paul's.

The house was quiet as she let herself in through the side-entrance, fastened Bobo's lead and led the little dog outside to where Lucy was waiting. There was a nip in the air, but at least it wasn't raining; they set off at a good pace, crossed into the park and took the usual path. They had reached a small clump of trees where the path curved abruptly when Bobo began to bark, and a moment later Brontes came hurtling round the corner, to leap up to greet Francesca, sniff at Lucy and turn his delighted attention to Bobo, who was yapping his small head off. They had come to a halt, not wishing to be bowled over by the warmth of the big dog's attention, which gave his master ample time to join them.

'Hello—what a pleasant morning.' He sounded as though they had met recently. Francesca knew exactly how long it had been since they had last met—ten days. She bade him good-morning in a chilly voice, and when he looked at Lucy she was forced to add, 'This is my sister, Lucy. Professor Pitt-Colwyn, Lucy.'

Lucy offered a hand. 'I hoped I'd meet you one day,' she told him, 'but of course you've been away. What do you do with your dog? Does he go with you?'

'If it's possible; otherwise he stays at home and gets spoilt. You like him?'

'He's gorgeous. We've got a cat and kittens;

I expect Francesca told you that—now the kittens are getting quite big we'll have to find homes for them.' She peeped at her sister's face; she looked cross. 'I'll take Bobo for a run—will Brontes come with me?'

'He'll be delighted. We'll stroll along to meet you.'

'We should be going back,' said Francesca, still very cool.

Lucy was already darting ahead and the professor appeared not to have heard her. 'I wish to talk to you, so don't be a silly girl and put on airs—'

'Well, really—' She stopped and looked up at his bland face. 'I am not putting on airs, and there is nothing for us to talk about.'

'You're very touchy—high time you left that job.' And at her indignant gasp he added, 'Just keep quiet and listen to me.'

He took her arm and began to walk after the fast retreating Lucy and the dogs. 'You would like to leave Lady Mortimor, would you not? I know of a job which might suit you. A close friend of mine died recently, leaving a widow and a small daughter. Eloise was an actress before she married—indeed, she has returned to the stage for short periods since their marriage—now she has the opportunity to go on tour with a play and is desperate to find someone to live in her house, run it for her and look after little Peggy while she is away. The tour is three or four months and then if it is successful they will go to a London theatre. You will have *carte blanche* and the services of a daily help in the house. No days off—but Peggy will be at school so that you should have a certain amount of free time. Peggy goes to a small day school, five minutes' walk from Cornel Mews—'

'That's near Lady Mortimor's—'

'Yes—don't interrupt. Eloise will come home for the very occasional weekend or day, but since the tour is largely in the north of England that isn't likely to be very often. The salary isn't bad ...' He mentioned a sum which left Francesca's pretty mouth agape.

'That's—that's ... just for a week? Are you sure? Lady Mortimor ... I'm not properly trained.'

'You don't need to be.' He looked down his commanding nose at her. 'Will you consider it?'

'It's not permanent—and what about the cat and her kittens?'

He said smoothly, 'It will last for several months, probably longer, and you will find it easy to find another similar post once you have a good reference.'

'Lady Mortimor won't give me one.'

'I am an old friend of Eloise; I imagine that my word will carry sufficient weight. As for the cat and kittens, they may come and live in my house; Brontes will love to have them.'

'Oh, but won't your—that is, anyone mind?'

'No. I shall be seeing Eloise later; may I tell her that you are willing to go and see her?'

'I would have liked time to think about it.'

'Well, you can have ten minutes while I round up the rest of the party.'

He had gone before she could protest, walking away from her with long, easy strides.

He had said 'ten minutes' and she suspected that he had meant what he had said. It sounded a nice job and the money was far beyond her wildest expectations, and she wouldn't be at anyone's beck and call.

Prudence told her that she was probably going out of the frying pan into the fire. On the other hand, nothing venture, nothing win. When he came back presently with Lucy chattering happily and a tired Bobo and a still lively Brontes in tow, she said at once, 'All right, I'll go and see this lady if you'll give me her address. Only it will have to be in the evening.'

'Seven o'clock tomorrow evening. Mrs Vincent, two, Cornel Mews. I'll let her know. I shan't be here tomorrow; I'll see you on Tuesday. You're free for the rest of the day?'

For one delighted moment she thought he was going to suggest that they should spend it together, but all he said was, 'Goodbye,' before he started to whistle to Brontes and turned on his heel, walking with the easy air of a man who had done what he had set out to do.

Lucy tucked an arm in hers. 'Now tell me

everything—why are you going to see this Mrs Vincent?'

They started to walk back and by the time they had reached the house Lucy knew all about it. They took Bobo into the kitchen and went back to their rooms to make some coffee and talk it over.

'It won't matter whether Mrs Vincent is nice or not if she's not going to be there,' observed Lucy. 'Oh, Fran, won't it be heavenly to have no one there but us—and Peggy of course—I wonder how old she is?'

'I forgot to ask...'

'All that money,' said Lucy dreamily. 'Now we can easily both get winter coats.'

'Well, I must save as much as I can. Supposing I can't find another job?'

'Never cross your bridges until you get to them,' said Lucy. 'Come on, let's go and look at the shops.' She put the kittens back in their box with their mother.

'I'm glad they'll all have a good home,' Francesca said.

'Yes. I wonder where it is?'

'Somewhere suitable for a professor,' said Francesca snappily. It still rankled that he had taken leave of her so abruptly. There was no reason why he shouldn't, of course. He had done his good deed for the day: found help for his friend and enabled her to leave Lady Mortimor's house.

'I shall enjoy giving her my notice,' she told Lucy.

* * *

It seemed as though Monday would never end but it did, tardily, after a day of Lady Mortimor's deep displeasure vented upon anyone and anything which came within her range, due to an early morning visit to her hairdresser who had put the wrong coloured streaks in her hair. Francesca had been ordered to make another appointment immediately so that this might be remedied at once, but unfortunately the hairdresser had no cancellations. Francesca, relaying this unwelcome news, had the receiver snatched from her and listened to her employer demanding the instant dismissal of the girl who had done her hair that morning, a demand which was naturally enough refused and added to Lady Mortimor's wrath.

'Why not get Ethel to shampoo your hair and re-set it?' Francesca suggested, and was told not to be so stupid, and after that there was no hope of doing anything right ... She was tired and a little cross by the time she got to their rooms to find Lucy ready with a pot of tea.

'You drink that up,' she told Francesca bracingly. 'Put on that brown jacket and skirt—I know they're old, but they're elegant—and do do your face.' She glanced at the clock. 'You've twenty minutes.'

It was exactly seven o'clock when she rang the bell of the charming little cottage in Cornel Mews. Its door was a rich dark red and there were bay trees in tubs on either side of it, and its one downstairs window was curtained in ruffled white net. She crossed her fingers for luck and took a deep breath as the door was opened.

The woman standing there was small and slim and as pretty as a picture. Her dark hair was in a fashionable tangle and she wore the kind of make-up it was difficult to separate from natural colouring. She wore a loose shirt over a very narrow short skirt and high-heeled suede boots and she could have been any age between twenty and thirty. She was in fact thirty-five.

'Miss Haley—do come in, Renier has told me all about you ...' She ushered Francesca into a narrow hall and opened a door into a surprisingly large living-room. 'Sit down and do have a drink while we get to know each other.'

Francesca sat, took the sherry she was offered and, since for the moment she had had no chance to say a word, she stayed silent.

'Did Renier explain?' asked Mrs Vincent. 'You know what men are, they never listen.'

It was time she said something, thought Francesca. 'He told me that you were going on tour and needed someone to look after your

38

daughter and keep house for you.'

'Bless the darling, he had it right.' Mrs Vincent curled up in a vast armchair with her drink. 'It's just the details—'

'You don't know anything about me,' protested Francesca.

'Oh, but I do, my daily woman is sister to Lady Mortimor's cook; besides, Renier said you were a sensible young woman with a sense of responsibility, and that's good enough for me. When can you come? I'm off at the end of next week.' She didn't give Francesca a chance to speak. 'Is the money all right? All the bills will go to my solicitor, who'll deal with them, and he'll send you a weekly cheque to cover household expenses and your salary. If you need advice or anything he'll deal with it.'

Francesca got a word in at last. 'Your daughter—how old is she? Can she meet me before I come? I have a sister who would have to live here with me.'

'That's fine. She's up in the nursery; I'll get her down.'

Mrs Vincent went out of the room and called up the narrow stairs, and presently a small girl came into the room. She was one of the plainest children Francesca had ever set eyes on: lank, pale hair, a long, thin face, small, dark eyes and an unhappy little mouth.

'She's six years old,' said Mrs Vincent in a detached way. 'Goes to school of course—very bright, so I've been told. Shake hands with

Miss Haley, Peggy. She's coming to stay with you while I'm away.'

The child shook hands with Francesca and Francesca kept the small paw in her own for a moment. 'I shall like coming here to live with you,' she said gently. 'I've a sister, too ...' She remembered something. 'Have you a cat or a dog to look after?'

The child shook her head. Her mother answered for her. 'My last nanny wouldn't have them in the house, though it's all one to me.' She laughed. 'I'm not here long enough to mind.'

'Then could I bring a kitten with me? Perhaps you would like one of your very own to look after, Peggy?'

The child smiled for the first time; there was an endearing gap in her teeth. 'For my own?' she asked.

'If your mother will allow that.'

'Oh, let the child have a pet if she wants.' Mrs Vincent added unexpectedly, 'She takes after her father.'

A remark which made everything clear to Francesca; a lovely, fragile creature like Mrs Vincent would find this plain, silent child a handicap now that she was going back on the stage. Probably she loved her dearly, but she wasn't going to let her interfere with her career. She went pink when Mrs Vincent said, 'I've been left comfortably off, but I've no intention of dwindling into a lonely widowhood,'

40

because she might have read her thoughts. She smiled suddenly. 'I shall wait for a decent interval and get married again.'

Francesca watched Peggy's small face; it was stony with misery. She said quickly, 'I'll bring the kitten when I come, shall I? And you can choose a name for it—it's a little boy cat; he's black and white with yellow eyes.'

Peggy slipped a small hand into hers. 'Really? Will he live here with us?'

'Of course, for this will be his home, won't it?'

Eloise poured herself another drink. 'You have no idea what a relief this is—may I call you Francesca? Now when can we expect you?'

'References?' ventured Francesca.

'Renier says you're OK. That's good enough for me; I told you that.'

'I shall have to give a week's notice to Lady Mortimor. I can do that tomorrow.'

'Good. I can expect you in a week's time. Give me a ring and let me know what time of day you'll be coming and I'll make a point of being in. Now have you time to go round the cottage with me?'

It was a small place, but very comfortably furnished with a well-planned kitchen and, on the ground floor, the living-room and, on the floor above, two good-sized bedrooms and a smaller room with a small bathroom leading from it. 'This is the nursery,' said Mrs Vincent. 'Peggy plays here—she's got masses of toys;

she's quite happy to amuse herself.'

Francesca wondered about that although she said nothing. 'How long will you be away?' she asked.

'Oh, my dear, how am I to know? The tour will last three months at least, and with luck will end up at a London theatre; if it doesn't I shall get my agent to find me something else.'

'Yes, of course. Has Peggy any grandparents or cousins who may want to visit?'

'My parents are in America; Jeff's live in Wiltshire, almost Somerset, actually. We don't see much of them.' Something in her voice stopped Francesca from asking any more questions, and presently she bade Mrs Vincent goodbye, and bent to shake Peggy's hand.

'You won't forget the kitten?'

'No, I'll bring him with me, I promise.'

Back in her little sitting-room she told Lucy everything: 'It's a dear little house, you'll love it. I think Peggy is lonely—she's withdrawn— perhaps she misses her father; I don't know how long ago he died. I promised her a kitten— the black and white one. Mrs Vincent didn't mind.'

'You don't like her much, do you?' asked Lucy shrewdly.

'Well, she's charming and friendly and easy-going, but she didn't seem very interested in Peggy. Perhaps it's hard to stay at home quietly with a small child if you've been used to theatre friends, and perhaps when her husband was alive they went out a lot.'

'It'll be better than Lady Mortimor's, anyway. We had better start packing up tomorrow, and don't forget Professor Pitt-Colwyn is going to take mother cat and the other kittens. Shall you meet him tomorrow?'

'He said he would be there.' She frowned. 'I must be careful what I say about Mrs Vincent; he said he was a close friend of her husband so I expect he is a close friend of hers as well.'

'Do you suppose she's got her eye on him?'

'Don't be vulgar, Lucy. I should think it was very likely, although for all we know he's married already.'

'You'd better ask him—'

'Indeed I will not.'

He was in the park, waiting for her when she got there the next morning with Bobo. It was a bright day with more than a hint of the coming winter's chill and Francesca, an elderly cardigan over her blouse and skirt, wished she had worn something warmer.

He wasted no time on good-mornings but said, 'You're cold; why didn't you wear something sensible? We had better walk briskly.'

He marched her off at a fine pace, with Bobo keeping up with difficulty and Brontes circling around them. 'Well? You saw Eloise Vincent? Are you going to take the job?'

'Yes, I'm going to give Lady Mortimor my notice this morning and let Mrs Vincent know when I'll be going to her.'

'You saw Peggy?'

'Yes.'

He looked down at her thoughtfully. 'And ...?'

'She's a quiet little girl, isn't she? I said I would take one of our kittens there for her to look after; her mother said that I might. You will take the mother cat and the other kittens, won't you?'

'Certainly I will. When will it be convenient for me to collect them? One evening? Let me see, I'm free on Thursday after six o'clock. Where exactly do you live?'

'Well, over the garage at the back of the house. There's a side-door; there's no knocker or bell, you just have to thump.'

'Then shall we say between six o'clock and half-past six? Have you a basket?'

'No, I'll get a cardboard box from the kitchen.'

'No need. I'll bring a basket with me. You're quite happy about this job?'

'Yes, thank you. You see, it's much more money and it will be so nice not to be ... that is, it will be nice to be on our own.'

'That I can well believe. Are you scared of Lady Mortimor?'

She gave his question careful thought. 'No, not in the least, but she is sometimes rather rude if anything has annoyed her. I have longed to shout back at her but I didn't dare—

she would have given me the sack.'

'Well, now you can bawl her out as much as you like, though I don't suppose you will; you've been too well brought up.'

He had spoken lightly, but when she looked at him she saw the mocking little smile. He must think her a spineless creature, dwindling into a dull spinsterhood. He had been kind, but his pity angered her. After all, she hadn't asked him for help. She said in her quiet voice, 'I have to go. Thank you for your help, and we'll have mother cat and the kittens ready for you when you come.' She gave him a stiff smile. 'Goodbye, Professor Pitt-Colwyn.'

She would contrive to be out when he called on Thursday evening, she decided as she made her way back to the house.

She couldn't have chosen a worse time in which to give in her notice. Lady Mortimor had been to a bridge party on the previous day and lost money, something she couldn't bear to do, and over and above that her dressmaker had telephoned to say that the dress she had wanted delivered that morning was not finished. Francesca went into the room in time to hear her employer declaring that it was no concern of hers if the girl working on it was ill, the dress was to be delivered by two o'clock that afternoon. She glanced up when she saw Francesca. 'Better still, I'll send round a girl to collect it and it had better be ready.

'You heard that,' she snapped. 'That stupid

woman having the cheek to say I can't have the dress today. I intend to wear it to the Smithers' drinks party this evening. You'll fetch it after lunch.'

She sat down at the little writing-table and glanced through the letters there. 'Bills,' she said peevishly. 'These tradespeople always wanting their money. You'd better see to them, I suppose, Francesca.' She got up. 'I've a hair appointment—see that they're ready for me when I get back.'

Francesca picked up the letters. 'Lady Mortimor, I wish to give you a week's notice as from today.' She laid an envelope on the desk. 'I have put it in writing.'

Lady Mortimor looked as though she had been hit on the head. Her eyes popped from her head, her mouth gaped. When she had her breath she said, 'What nonsense is this? You must be mad, girl. A cushy job and a flat of your own ... I won't hear of it.'

'There's nothing you can do about it,' Francesca pointed out reasonably. 'It isn't a cushy job, it's very badly paid, and it surely isn't a flat—it's two small rooms with a minute kitchen and a shower which doesn't work half the time.'

'You'll have difficulty in getting work, I'll see to that. I'll not give you a reference.'

'That won't be necessary. I already have a job to go to and your reference won't be required.'

46

'Then you can go now, do you hear, you ungrateful girl?'

'Just as you say, Lady Mortimor. You will have to give me two weeks' wages, one in lieu of notice.' She watched her employer's complexion becoming alarmingly red. 'And whom shall I ask to arrange the dinner party for Saturday? And your lunch party on Sunday? Shall I let Ethel have the bills to check? And there will be the invitations for the charity tea party you are giving next week.'

Francesca paused for breath, astonished at herself. Really she had been most unpleasant and deserved to be thrown out of the house for rudeness. She realised that she wouldn't mind that in the least.

Lady Mortimor knew when she was worsted. 'You will remain until the following week.'

'Tuesday evening,' Francesca interpolated gently, ignoring the woman's glare.

'You will send an advertisement to the usual papers this morning. I require letters in the first instance; interviews can be arranged later to suit me.'

'Certainly, Lady Mortimor. Am I to state the salary?'

'No. The flat goes with the job, of course.' She swept to the door. 'It may interest you to know that you have ruined my day. Such ingratitude has cut me to the quick.'

Francesca forbore from saying that, for
47

someone of Lady Mortimor's ample, corseted figure, the cut would have to be really deep.

Naturally a kind girl and seldom critical of other people, she felt guilty once she was alone. She had been most dreadfully rude; she felt thoroughly ashamed of herself. She had almost finished the bills when Maisie came in with her coffee.

'Cor, miss, what a lark—you going away. Mr Crow was just in the hall passing as you might say and 'eard it all. He said as 'ow you gave as good as you got and good luck to you, we all says—treated you something shameful, she 'as, and you a lady and all.'

'Why, Maisie, how very kind of you all. I'm afraid I was very rude...'

'A bit of plain speaking never 'urt no one, miss. I 'opes 'owever that 'oever takes yer place is capable of a bit of talking back.'

Francesca drank her coffee, feeling cheerful again. She wasn't going to apologise, but she would behave as she always had done, however unpleasant Lady Mortimor might choose to be.

She chose to be very unpleasant. It was a good thing that there were no signs of the professor the next morning for she might have burst into tears all over him and wallowed in self-pity, but by Thursday evening she didn't care any more and allowed Lady Mortimor's ill temper and spiteful remarks to flow over her head. Heedful of her decision, she took care

48

not to get to the rooms until well after seven o'clock, only to find the professor sitting in comfort in the only easy-chair in the place, drinking tea from a mug while Brontes brooded in a fatherly fashion over mother cat and the kittens in their box.

'There you are,' said Lucy as Francesca went in. 'We thought you'd never come. There's still tea in the pot. But Renier's eaten all the biscuits; he didn't have time for lunch. Have you had a beastly day?'

'Well, a bit sticky. I say, isn't Brontes sweet?'

The professor had got up from his chair and pushed her gently into it, and had gone to sit on the small wooden chair which creaked under his weight. He said now, 'I shall be away for the next ten days or so; I hope you settle down with Peggy.' His hooded gaze swept over her tired face. 'It's time you had a change, and I think you will find she will be much nicer to live with than your Lady Mortimor.' He got up. 'I must be going.' He scooped the cat and kittens into the basket he had brought with him, while Lucy cuddled the other kitten on her lap. 'I'll take good care of them,' he said. He smiled at them both. '*Tot ziens.*' And when Francesca made an effort to rise he said, 'No, I'll see myself out.'

The room seemed very empty once he had gone.

CHAPTER THREE

The week seemed never-ending, and Lady Mortimor was determined to get the last ounce of work out of Francesca before she left. There had been several answers to the advertisement, but so far the applicants had refused the job. They had turned up their noses at the so-called flat and two of them had exploded with laughter when they had been told their salary. They were, they had pointed out, secretary-companions, not dog minders or errand girls. Lady Mortimor actually had been shaken. 'You will have to remain until someone suitable can take your place,' she had said the day before Francesca was due to leave.

'That won't be possible,' said Francesca. 'I start my new job immediately I leave here. One of the agencies might have help for you, but only on a daily or weekly basis.'

Lady Mortimor glared at her. 'I am aware of that, but I have no intention of paying the exorbitant fees they ask.' She hesitated. 'I am prepared to overlook your rudeness, Francesca. I am sure that you could arrange to go to this new job, say, in a week's time?'

'I am very sorry, Lady Mortimor, but that is impossible.'

She watched her employer sweep out of the room in a towering rage, and went back to making out the last of the cheques for the tradesmen.

The last day was a nightmare she refused to dwell upon. Lady Mortimor gave her not a moment to herself, and when six o'clock came declared that half the things she had told Francesca to do were still not done. Francesca listened quietly, allowing the tirade to flow over her head. 'There is nothing of importance left to do,' she pointed out. 'Whoever can come in place of me can deal with anything I've overlooked. Goodbye, Lady Mortimor.'

She closed the door quietly on her erstwhile employer's angry voice. She had a happier send-off from the staff, and Crow presented her with a potted plant from them all and wished her well. 'For we're all sure you deserve it, miss,' he said solemnly.

She went to join Lucy, and, after a meal, packed the last of their belongings. A taxi would take them the short distance to Cornel Mews in the morning.

Eloise Vincent was waiting for them when they arrived mid-morning. Peggy was at school, she told them. 'My daily woman will fetch her after lunch. I'm up to my eyes packing; I'm off this evening. I've written down all the names and addresses you might need and a phone number in case you should need me urgently, but for heaven's sake don't ring unless it's something dire.' She led the way upstairs. 'You each have a room; I'll leave you

51

to unpack.' She glanced at the cat basket Lucy was holding. 'Is this the kitten? I dare say Peggy will like having him. There's coffee in the kitchen; help yourselves, will you? Lucy's bed is made up. I'm sorry I haven't put clean sheets on the other bed; the room's been turned out, but I had to empty cupboards and drawers—you won't mind doing it?'

She smiled charmingly and went downstairs, leaving them to inspect their new quarters. The rooms were prettily furnished and to have a room of one's own would be bliss. They unpacked and hung everything away and, with the kitten still in his basket, went downstairs. Mrs Wells, the daily cleaner, was in the kitchen. She was a pleasant-faced, middle-aged woman who poured coffee for them, found a saucer of milk for the kitten and offered to do anything to help. 'I've been here quite a while, before poor Dr Vincent died, so I know all there is to know about the place. I come in the mornings—eight o'clock—and go again after lunch,' she offered biscuits, 'though I said I'd fetch Peggy from school before I go home today.'

'Can't we do that?' asked Francesca. 'We have to get to know her, and it's a chance to see where the school is.'

'Well, now, that would be nice. It's at the end of Cornel Road, just round the corner in Sefton Park Street. Mrs Vincent hoped you wouldn't mind having a snack lunch—the fridge is well stocked and you can cook this evening. She is going out to lunch with a friend, but she'll be back by two o'clock and aims to leave around six o'clock—being fetched by car.'

Francesca thought of the questions she wanted answered before Mrs Vincent left. She put down her coffee-cup. 'Perhaps I could talk to her now?'

Eloise Vincent was in the sitting-room, sitting at her desk, a telephone book before her, the receiver in her hand. She looked up and smiled as Francesca went in. 'Settling in?' she asked. 'Mrs Wells is a fount of knowledge if you've any questions.'

'Yes. She's been most helpful. Mrs Vincent, could you spare a moment? Just to tell me what time Peggy goes to bed, if there's anything she won't eat, which friends is she allowed to play with while you are away...?'

'Oh, dear, what a lot of questions. She goes to bed about seven o'clock, I suppose. She eats her dinner at school and I've been giving her tea about five o'clock. I don't know about her friends. My husband used to take her with him when he went to see his friends; they haven't been here, although on her birthday we had a party, of course—'

'May I have the names of your doctor and dentist?'

Mrs Vincent laughed. 'Oh, get Renier if anything is worrying you. He's Peggy's godfather; he's fond of her. She's never ill, anyway. Now, you really must excuse me—Mrs Wells can tell you anything else you may want to know.'

It was obvious to Francesca that Mrs Vincent had no more time for her. She went back to the kitchen and did a thorough tour of its cupboards and shelves, went through the linen cupboard with Mrs Wells and, when Mrs Vincent had left for her lunch appointment, sat down with Mrs Wells and Lucy to eat sandwiches and drink more coffee.

Peggy came out of school at three o'clock, and both of them went to fetch her since Mrs Vincent wasn't back. The children came out in twos and threes and Peggy was one of the last, walking slowly and alone.

They went to meet her and she seemed pleased to see them, walking between them, holding their hands, answering their cheerful questions about school politely. Only when Francesca said, 'The kitten's waiting for you,' did she brighten. They spent the rest of the short walk discussing suitable names for him.

Mrs Vincent was back and there was a car before the door, which was being loaded with her luggage by a tall, middle-aged man. He said, 'Hello, Peggy,' without stopping what he was doing.

She said, 'Hello, Mr Seymour,' in a small wooden voice, all her animation gone again.

'You'd better go and say goodbye to your

mother,' he told her over his shoulder. 'We're off in a few minutes.'

The three of them went inside and found Mrs Vincent in the sitting-room, making a last-minute phone call. 'Darlings,' she cried in her light, pretty voice, 'I'm going now. Come and say goodbye to your old mother, Peggy, and promise to be a good girl while I'm away. I'll send you lots of postcards and when I can I will telephone to you.' She kissed her small daughter and turned to Francesca. 'I'll be trying to keep in touch,' she said. 'I'm sure you'll do a marvellous job. Let me know how you are getting on from time to time.'

She smiled, looking so pretty and appealing that Francesca smiled back, quelling the uneasy feeling that Eloise Vincent was only too delighted to be starting her theatrical career once more and couldn't wait to get away.

She was prepared for Peggy's tears once her mother had gone, but the child's face had remained impassive. 'May I have the kitten now?' she asked, almost before they were out of sight.

She and the small creature took to each other at once. She sat happily in the sitting-room with him on her small, bony knees, talking to him and stroking his head with a small, gentle hand. 'I shall call him Tom,' she told Francesca.

'That's a nice name.'

'Daddy used to read me a story about Tom

Kitten …' The small voice quavered and Francesca said quickly, 'Shall we talk about your daddy? I'd like to know all about him.'

So that was the trouble, she reflected, listening to the child's rambling description of her father and the fun they had had together. Peggy had loved him dearly and there had been no one to talk to her about him. She let the child chat on, the small face animated, and then said gently, 'What nice things you have to remember about him, Peggy, and of course he'll never go away; he'll always be there inside your head.'

'I like you,' said Peggy.

It took a few days to settle into a routine. Lucy went to school each morning and Francesca took Peggy to her school shortly afterwards, going back to make the beds and shop and wash and iron while Mrs Wells gave the house what she called a good tidy up. Tom settled down without any nonsense, aware by now that he belonged to Peggy and no one else, sitting beside her chair at meals and sleeping at the foot of her bed.

There had been no news of Mrs Vincent. Francesca wasn't sure where she was, for the promised list of the various towns the company would be appearing in hadn't turned up. It was a relief that at the end of the week there was a cheque in the post with her salary and a housekeeping allowance.

It was two days later, after they had had tea

and Francesca was on the floor in the kitchen, showing Peggy how to play marbles while Tom pranced around them both, that the front doorbell was rung.

'I'll go,' called Lucy, in the sitting-room with her homework, and a moment later Professor Pitt-Colwyn's voice sent Peggy flying to the kitchen door. He caught her in his arms and kissed her soundly. 'Hello, love, I thought it was time I came to see how you were getting on...'

He watched Francesca get up off the floor and brush down her skirt. 'Marbles—am I in time for a game?' and then he added, 'good evening, Francesca.'

She was surprised at how glad she was to see him. 'Good evening, Professor.' She scanned his face and saw that he was tired. 'Shall we go into the sitting-room? I'll make a cup of coffee while you and Peggy have a talk—she wants to show you Tom.'

He looked down at the small, earnest face staring up at him. 'A splendid idea—shall we be disturbing Lucy?'

'I've just finished,' said Lucy. 'I'll help Fran get the coffee—'

'A sandwich with it?' asked Francesca.

'That would be very nice.'

'Have you had no lunch or tea?'

'A rather busy day.' He smiled, and she could see that he wasn't going to talk about it.

She made a pot of coffee, cut a plateful of

cold beef sandwiches and bore the tray into the sitting-room. Peggy was sitting on the professor's knee and Tom had curled up on her small lap. Francesca was astonished to hear the child's happy voice, talking nineteen to the dozen.

'We are talking about Peggy's father,' said the professor deliberately.

Francesca said at once, 'He must have been a marvellous dad. Peggy has told us a little about him.' She poured him a cup and gave it to him. 'You stay there, darling. Here's your milk, and take care not to spill it over your godfather's trousers.'

She passed the sandwiches too, and watched him eat the lot. 'There's a cake I made this afternoon,' she suggested.

He ate several slices of that too, listening to Peggy's chatter, knowing just when to make some remark to make her giggle. Francesca let her bedtime go by, for the little girl was really happy. It was the professor who said at last, 'It's way past your bedtime, Peggy,' and when she wound her arms round his neck he said, 'if you go to bed like the good girl you are, I'll come and take you to the zoo on Saturday afternoon.'

'Fran and Lucy too?'

'Of course. Tom can mind the house and we'll come back here and have an enormous tea.'

She slid off his knee. Kissed him goodnight

then, and went to stand by Francesca's chair. 'Will we?' she asked. 'Will we, really?'

'If your godfather says so, then of course we will, and I'll make a simply enormous cake and we'll have crumpets dripping with butter.'

'Could Lucy put her to bed?' asked the professor. 'We might have a chat?'

'Of course I can.' Lucy scooped up the kitten and handed him to Peggy. 'And Fran will come and tuck you up when you're in bed.'

Peggy went happily enough, her hand in Lucy's and the kitten tucked under one arm. Francesca, suddenly shy, offered more coffee.

'Any problems?' asked the professor.

She thought before she answered. 'No, I don't think so. I should have liked to have known a bit more about Peggy before Mrs Vincent left, but there wasn't much time. Mrs Wells is a great help with things like shopping and so on. Peggy doesn't seem to have any friends ... do you suppose it would be all right if I invited one or two children for tea one day? I think she is a very shy little girl.'

'She is a very unhappy little girl. She loved her father very much and she misses him; she likes to talk about him. I think that Eloise didn't understand that and the child is too small to carry so much hidden grief.' He glanced at her. 'She told me that she talks to you and Lucy about him.'

'Yes, he is still alive to her, isn't he? If you're sure that's the right thing to do?'

'Quite sure. By all means see if you can get some children round to play with her. Has she no friends at all at school?'

'Oh, one or two speak to her but she doesn't seem to have any special friends, but I'll do my best. She has masses of toys and it would be nice if she were to share them.'

'Have you heard from Eloise?'

'Me? No. She said she would be too busy rehearsing to write for a while.'

'I'm going to Cheltenham to see the opening show next week. If you think of anything you want to know about, let me know before then.'

'Thank you. She left everything beautifully organised. I expect she's a very good actress?'

He didn't answer, and she wondered uncomfortably if she had said something about Mrs Vincent which might have annoyed him. She couldn't think of anything but if he was in love with her, and she supposed that he was, he would be touchy about her. Lucy came in then.

'Peggy's bathed and in bed; she's waiting for you to say goodnight—both of you.'

The child wreathed her arms round Francesca's neck. 'I love you, Fran.'

'Thank you, darling. I love you too, and Tom of course. Now go to sleep quickly, won't you? Because he's asleep already.'

The professor was hugged in his turn, and he was reminded of his promise to take them to the zoo on Saturday, then he was kissed goodnight. 'Now tuck me in, please, Fran.'

So she was tucked in and he stood in the little room, leaning against the wall, watching, his eyes half closed.

Back in the sitting-room he said, 'I must be off. Thanks for the coffee and sandwiches.'

'It made Peggy very happy to see you,' Francesca said. The thought that it had made her very happy too was sternly dismissed. 'You will have a good meal before you go to bed, won't you?'

He looked as though he were going to laugh. 'Indeed I will.' He smiled at Lucy and dropped a large hand on Francesca's shoulder for a moment and went away. Lucy went to the window to watch him drive away, but Francesca busied herself with the cups and saucers.

'I shall enjoy the zoo,' said Lucy.

'Yes, it should be fun; Peggy will love it. Lucy, I must do something about finding her some friends...'

'Well, gossip around when you go to get her from school. I dare say our Eloise discouraged them—children are noisy and they make a mess...'

'You're probably right, but don't call her that, dear—we might forget and say something—I mean, I think he's in love with her, don't you? He's going all the way to Cheltenham for the opening night.'

They were in the kitchen, washing up the coffee-cups.

'That doesn't mean that he's in love with her. What shall we have for supper? It's a bit late.'

The following day Francesca made a few tentative overtures to the mothers and nannies taking the children to school. They were friendly enough, and she made a point of letting them know that Mrs Vincent had gone away for a time and that she was looking after Peggy. She said no more than that, but it was, she thought, the thin end of the wedge...

She wasn't sure, but she thought that maybe the children had been discouraged from getting friendly with Peggy, a child too shy to assert herself with the making of friends. It might take some time, but it would be nice if she could get to know a few children while her mother was away, so that by the time she got back home Peggy would have established a circle of little friends. Already the child was livelier, learning to play the games small children played, spending long hours with Francesca or Lucy rearranging the elaborate doll's house, planning new outfits for the expensive dolls she had. 'Woollies for the winter,' explained Francesca, getting knitting needles and wool and starting on miniature sweaters and cardigans.

They all went shopping the next day, and it was apparent that Peggy had never been to Woolworth's. They spent a long time there while she trotted from one counter to the other, deciding how to spend the pocket money

Francesca had given her. After the rigours of Lady Mortimor's household, life was very pleasant. Francesca, going about her chores in the little house, planning meals, playing with Peggy, sitting in the evenings sewing or knitting, with Lucy doing her homework at the table, felt that life was delightful. They had a home, well, not a permanent one, but still a home for the time being—enough money, the prospect of having some new clothes and of adding to their tiny capital at the bank. She was almost content.

The professor came for them after lunch on Saturday, bundled them briskly into his car, and drove to the zoo. It was a mild autumn day, unexpected after several days of chilly rain. Francesca, in her good suit, her burnished hair gleaming in the sunshine, sat beside him in the car making polite small talk, while Lucy and Peggy in the back giggled and chattered together. The professor, who had been up most of the night with a very ill patient, allowed the happy chatter from the back seat to flow over his tired head and listened to Francesca's pretty voice, not hearing a word she said but enjoying the sound of it.

The afternoon was a success; they wandered along, stopping to look at whatever caught their eyes, with Peggy skipping between them until she caught sight of the camels, who were padding along with their burden of small children.

The professor fished some money out of his pocket and gave it to Lucy. 'You two have a ride; Francesca and I are going to rest our feet. We'll be here when you get back.'

'You make me feel very elderly—bunions and dropped arches and arthritic knees,' protested Francesca, laughing as they sat down on an empty bench.

'You, my dear girl, will never be elderly. That is an attitude of mind.' He spoke lightly, not looking at her. 'You have settled down quite happily, I hope?'

'Oh, yes, and Lucy and Peggy get on famously.'

'So I have noticed. And you, Francesca, you mother them both.'

She was vexed to feel her cheeks grow hot. She asked stiffly, 'How is Brontes? And mother cat and the kittens?'

'He has adopted them. You must come and see them. The children are at school during the day? You will be free for lunch one day? I'll give you a ring.'

'Is that an invitation?' asked Francesca frostily.

'Certainly it is. You want to come, don't you?'

She had no intention of saying so. 'I shall be very glad to see mother cat and the kittens again.'

His stern mouth twitched a little. 'I shall be there too; I hope you will be glad to see me.'

'Well, of course.' She opened her handbag and looked inside and closed it again for something to do. She would be very glad to see him again, only he mustn't be allowed to know that. He was merely being friendly, filling in his days until Eloise Vincent should return. She wished that she knew more about him; she voiced the wish without meaning to and instantly wanted it unsaid.

'You flatter me.' He told her blandly, 'Really there is nothing much to tell. I work—as most men work. Perhaps I am fortunate in liking that work.'

'Do you go to a hospital every day or have a surgery?'

'I go to several hospitals and I have consulting-rooms.'

She persisted. 'If you are a professor, do you teach the students?'

'Yes. To the best of my ability!' He added gently, 'I examine them too, and from time to time I travel. Mostly to examine students in hospitals in other countries. I have a very competent secretary and a nurse to help me—'

'I'm sorry, I've been very rude; I can't think why I asked you about your work or—or anything.' She had gone pink again and she wouldn't look at him, so that the long, curling lashes, a shade darker than her hair, lay on her cheeks. She looked quite beautiful and he studied her with pleasure, saying nothing. It was a great relief to her when Lucy and Peggy came running towards them. Caught up in the excited chatter from Peggy, she forgot the awkward moment.

They went back to the little house in the Mews presently and had their tea: fairy cakes and a gingerbread, little sandwiches and chocolate biscuits. 'It's like my birthday,' said Peggy, her small, plain face wreathed in smiles.

The professor stayed for an hour after tea, playing ludo on the floor in front of the sitting-room fire. When he got to his feet, towering over them, he observed pleasantly, 'A very nice afternoon—we must do it again some time.' He kissed his small god-daughter, put a friendly arm around Lucy's shoulders, and went to the door with Francesca.

'I'll phone you,' was all he said, 'and thanks for the tea.'

*　　　*　　　*

It was several days later when she had a phone call. A rather prim voice enquired if she were Miss Haley and went on to ask if she would lunch with Professor Pitt-Colwyn in two days' time. 'If it wouldn't inconvenience you,' went on the voice, 'would you go to the Regent hospital at noon and ask for the professor?'

Francesca agreed. Were they going to eat at the hospital? she wondered, and what should she wear? It would have to be the brown suit again. Her winter coat was too shabby and although there was some money now Lucy needed a coat far more than she did. She would wash her hair and do her nails, she decided, and buy a new lipstick.

The Regent hospital was in the East End. It was a hideous building, heavily embellished with fancy brickwork of the Victorian era, brooding over a network of shabby streets. Francesca got off the bus opposite its entrance and presented herself at the reception desk inside the entrance hall.

The clerk appeared to know who she was, for she lifted the phone and spoke into it, and a moment later beckoned to one of the porters.

'If you would wait for a few minutes, Miss Haley, the porter will show you...'

Francesca followed the man, wishing that she hadn't come; she couldn't imagine the professor in this vast, echoing building. Probably he had forgotten that he had invited her and was deep in some highly urgent operation. Come to think of it, she didn't know if he was a surgeon or a physician. She sat down in a small room at the back of the entrance hall, facing a long corridor. It was empty and after a minute or two she was tempted to get up and go home, but all at once there were people in it, walking towards her: the professor, towering above the posse of people trying to keep up with him, a short, stout ward sister, two or three young men in short white coats, an older man in a long white coat, a tall, stern-looking woman with a pile of folders under one arm and, bringing up the rear, a worried-looking nurse carrying more folders.

The professor paused in the doorway of the room she was in, filling it entirely with his bulk. 'Ah, there you are,' he observed in a voice which suggested that she had been in hiding and he had just discovered her. 'Give me five minutes...'

He had gone and everyone else with him, jostling each other to keep up.

He reappeared not ten minutes later, elegant in a dark grey suit and a silk tie which had probably cost as much as her best shoes. They had been her best for some time now, and she hardly ever wore them for they pinched abominably.

'Kind of you to come here,' he told her breezily. 'I wasn't sure of the exact time at which I could be free. Shall we go?'

She walked beside him, out to the space reserved for consultants' cars and got into the car, easing her feet surreptitiously out of her shoes. The professor, watching out of the corner of his eye, turned a chuckle into a cough and remarked upon the weather.

He drove west, weaving his way through the small side-streets until she, quite bewildered by the one-way traffic, saw that they were in Shaftesbury Avenue. But only briefly; he turned into side-streets again and ten minutes or so later turned yet again into a narrow street, its trees bare of leaves now, the houses on either side elegant Regency, each with a very small garden before it, steps leading up to doorways topped by equally elegant fanlights. The professor stopped the car and got out to open her door. 'I thought we might lunch at home,' he told her. 'Brontes is anxious to see you again.'

'You live here?' asked Francesca. A silly question, but she had been surprised; it was, she guessed, five minutes away from Mrs Vincent's cottage.

'Yes.' He took her arm and marched her up the steps as the door was opened by a dignified middle-aged man in a black jacket and pin-striped trousers.

'Ah, Peak. Francesca, this is Peak, who sees that this place runs on oiled wheels. Mrs Peak is my housekeeper. Peak, this is Miss Haley. Show her where she can leave her coat, will you?' He picked up his bag. 'I'll be in the drawing-room, Francesca.'

In the charming little cloakroom concealed beneath the curving staircase, she poked at her hair, added more lipstick and deplored the suit; she had better take off the jacket otherwise it might look as though she were ready to dart out of the house again. Her blouse wasn't new either, but it was ivory silk, laundered and pressed with great care, and the belt around her slender waist was soft leather. Her feet still hurt, but she would be able to ease them out of her shoes again once they were sitting at the table. She went back into the narrow hall and the professor appeared at a half-open door.

'Come and have a drink before lunch.' He held the door wide and Brontes stuck his great head round it, delighted to see her.

The room was long and narrow, with a bay window overlooking the street and a charming Adam fireplace. The chairs were large and deep and well cushioned, and there was a scattering of small lamp tables as well as a handsome bow-fronted display cabinet embellished with marquetry, its shelves filled with silver and porcelain. The professor went to the rent table under the window. He asked, 'Sherry for you? And do sit down.'

She sat, and was aware that mother cat and her kittens were cosily curled up together in one of the easy chairs. She said, 'Oh, they seem very much at home.'

He handed her the sherry. 'Brontes has seen to that; he is their devoted guardian angel.'

She sipped her sherry, very aware of him sitting opposite her, Brontes pressed up against him, both of them watching her. Her tongue, as it sometimes did, ran away with her. 'Do you want to tell me something? Is that why you asked me to lunch?'

'Yes, to both your questions, but it can wait.' He settled back in his great chair. 'Your sister is a bright child; has she any ideas about the future?' It was a casual question and she answered readily enough.

'She's clever; she's set her heart on GCSEs, A levels, and a university.'

'Some discerning young man will snap her up long before then.' He smiled at her. 'And why aren't you married?'

It was unexpected. 'Well, I—I ... that is, they weren't the right ones. None of them the right man.'

This muddled statement he received with a gentle smile. 'Have you any messages for Eloise?'

'If you would tell her that Peggy seems happy and is doing well at school and that everything is fine. She hasn't written or phoned, but I expect she's very busy.'

'Undoubtedly,' he agreed gravely. Peak came then to tell them that lunch was ready, and she went with the professor to a smaller room at the back of the house, which overlooked a surprisingly large garden. 'You've got trees, how lovely,' she exclaimed. 'It must look beautiful in the spring.'

They lunched off iced melon, baked salmon in a pastry case and a coffee *bavarois* and, while they ate, the professor kept the conversation quite firmly in his hands; impersonal topics, the kind of talk one might have had with a stranger sharing one's table in a restaurant, thought Francesca peevishly. Back in the drawing-room, drinking coffee from paper-thin cups, she said suddenly, 'I wish you would talk about your work—you looked different at the hospital; it's a side of you that I know nothing about.' She put down her cup. 'I'm sorry, I'm being nosy again.' She looked at her feet, aching in the shoes she longed to kick off. 'Only I'm interested,' she mumbled.

'I have an appointment at half-past two,' he told her. 'I'll drive you back as I go to my rooms, which means that we have half an hour. Do take off those shoes and curl up comfortably.'

'Oh, how did you know? I don't wear them very often and they're a bit tight. You don't mind?'

'Not in the least. What do you want to know about my work, Francesca?'

'Well, I know that you're a professor and a consultant, but are you a surgeon or a physician? You said you went to other hospitals and that you travelled. Why?'

'I'm a surgeon, open-heart surgery—valve replacements, by-passes, transplants. Most of my work is at Regent's, but I operate at all the big provincial hospitals if I'm needed. I have a private practice and an out-patients clinic twice a week. I work in Leiden too, occasionally in Germany and the States, and from time to time in the Middle East.'

'Leiden,' said Francesca. 'You said "*tot ziens*" one morning in the park; we looked it up—it's Dutch.'

72

'My mother is a Dutchwoman; she lives just outside Leiden. I spend a good deal of time there. My father was British; he died two years ago.'

He looked at her, half smiling, one eyebrow raised in a gentle way. The half-smile widened and she thought it was mocking, and went red. He must think her a half-wit with no manners. She plunged into a muddled speech. 'I don't know why I had to be so rude, I do apologise, I have no excuse, if I were you I wouldn't want to speak to me again—'

He said gently, 'But I'm not you, and fortunately I see no reason why I shouldn't speak to you again. For one thing, it may be necessary from time to time. I did tell Eloise that I would keep an eye on Peggy.'

'Yes, of course. I—I expect that you would like to go now.' She sat up straight and crammed her feet back into her shoes and then stood up. 'Thank you for my lunch—it was delicious.'

He appeared not to notice how awkward she felt. Only as he stopped in Cornel Mews and got out to take the key from her and open the door of the cottage did he say, 'We must have another talk some time, Francesca,' and he bent to kiss her cheek as she went past him into the hall.

CHAPTER FOUR

Francesca was sitting by the fire, reading to Peggy, when Lucy came in. 'Well, did you have a good lunch? What did you eat?'

Francesca recited the menu.

'Nice—to think I was chewing on liver and bacon ... Where did you go?'

'To his house; it's quite close by.'

Lucy flung down her school books and knelt down by the fire. 'Tell me everything,' she demanded.

When Francesca had finished she said, 'He must be very rich. I expect he's clever too. I wonder what his mum's like.'

'How's school?'

'OK.' Lucy dug into a pocket. 'There's a letter for you, but don't take any notice of it; I don't want to go ...'

The words were bravely said but palpably not true. A party of pupils was being organised to go skiing two weeks before Christmas. Two weeks in Switzerland with proper tuition and accompanied by teachers. The fare and the expenses totalled a sum which Francesca had no hope of finding.

'Oh, Lucy, I'm so sorry. If it's any consolation I'll get the money by hook or by crook for next winter.' She glanced at her sister's resolutely cheerful face. 'All your friends are going?'

'Well, most of them, but I really don't mind, Fran. We can have a lovely time here, getting ready for Christmas.'

So nothing more was said about it, although Francesca sat up late, doing sums which, however hard she tried, never added up to enough money to pay for Lucy's skiing holiday. There was enough money set aside for her school fees, of course, but that wasn't to be touched. She went to bed finally with a headache.

There was no postcard from Mrs Vincent; nor was there a phone call. Francesca reminded herself that the professor would be with her, and most likely he would bring back something for Peggy when he returned. The child showed no concern at the absence of news from her mother, although it seemed to Francesca that she was looking pale and seemed listless; even Tom's antics were met with only a half-hearted response. Francesca consulted Mrs Wells. 'I think she should see a doctor. She isn't eating much either. I wonder if she's missing her mother...'

Mrs Wells gave her an old-fashioned look. 'I'm not one for telling tales out of school, but 'er mum never 'as had no time for 'er. Disappointed she was; she so pretty and charming and Peggy as plain as a pikestaff. No, you don't need to fret yerself about that, Miss Haley; little Peggy don't love 'er mum all that much. She was 'appier when her granny and grandpa came to visit. That was when Dr Vincent was alive—loved the child they did, and she loved them.'

So Francesca had done nothing for a few more days, although Peggy didn't seem any better. She had made up her mind to get a doctor by now. If only the professor had phoned, she could have asked his advice, but he, of course, would be wherever Mrs Vincent was. She fetched Peggy from school, gave her her tea which she didn't want and, as soon as Lucy came home, took the child upstairs to bed. Peggy felt hot and she wished she could take her temperature, but there was a singular lack of first-aid equipment in the house, and she blamed herself for not having attended to that. She sat the child on her lap and started to undress her, and as she took off her clothes she saw the rash. The small, thin back was covered with red spots. She finished the undressing, washed the pale little face, and brushed the mousy hair and tucked the child up in bed. 'A nice glass of cold milk,' she suggested, 'and Lucy shall bring it up to you.'

'Tom—I want Tom,' said Peggy in a small voice. 'I've got a pain in my head.'

'You shall have Tom, my dear,' said Francesca and sped downstairs, told Lucy, and went to the phone. Even if the professor were still away, surely that nice man Peak would have a phone number or, failing that, know of a local doctor.

She dialled the number Mrs Vincent had left in her desk and Peak answered.

'Peak, did Professor Pitt-Colwyn leave a phone number? I need to speak to him—Peggy's ill.'

'A moment, Miss Haley,' and a second later the professor's voice, very calm, sounded in her ear.

'Francesca?'

'Oh, so you are there,' she said fiercely. 'Peggy's ill; there's a rash all over her back and she feels sick and listless. She's feverish, but I can't find a thermometer anywhere and I don't know where there's a doctor and I've not heard a word since Mrs Vincent went away—'

'Peggy's in bed? Good. I'll be with you in about ten minutes.' He rang off and she spent a moment with the unhappy thought that she had been anything but calm and sensible; she had even been rather rude ... and he had sounded impassive and impersonal, as though she were a patient to be dealt with efficiently. Though I'm not the patient, she thought in a muddled way as she went back to Peggy and sent Lucy downstairs to open the door for the professor, and then sat down on the side of the bed to hold the tearful child in her arms.

She didn't hear him come in; for such a big man he was both quick and silent. She was only aware of him when he put two hands on her shoulders and eased her away from Peggy and

77

took her place.

He was unhurried and perfectly calm and apparently unworried and it was several minutes before he examined the child, took her temperature and then sat back while Francesca made her comfortable again. 'Have you had chicken-pox?' He glanced at Francesca.

'Me? Oh, yes, years ago; so has Lucy.'

'And so have I, and now so has Peggy.' He took the small, limp hand in his. 'You'll feel better very soon, Peggy. Everyone has chicken-pox, you know, but it only lasts a few days. You will take the medicine Francesca will give you and then you'll sleep as soundly as Tom and in the morning I'll come and see you again.'

'I don't want Mummy to come home—'

'Well, love, there really is no need. Francesca will look after you, and as soon as you feel better we'll decide what is to happen next, shall we?' He kissed the hot little head. 'Lucy will come and sit with you until Francesca brings your medicine. *Tot ziens.*'

Peggy managed a watery smile and said, '*Tot ziens.*'

In the sitting-room Francesca asked anxiously, 'She's not ill, is she? I mean, ill enough to let her mother know? She said she didn't want to be—that is, there was no need to ring her unless there was something serious.'

When he didn't answer she added, 'I'm sorry if I was rude on the phone; I was worried and I

78

thought you were away.'

'Now why should you think that?'

'You said you were going to Cheltenham.'

'As indeed I did go.' He was writing a prescription as he spoke. 'Don't worry, Peggy is quite all right. She has a temperature but, having chicken-pox, that is only to be expected. Get this tomorrow morning and see that she takes it three times a day.' He took a bottle from his bag and shook out a tablet. 'This will dissolve in hot milk; it will make her more comfortable and she should sleep.'

He closed his bag and stood up. 'I'll call in on my way to the hospital in the morning, but if you're worried don't hesitate to phone me; I'll come at once.' At the door he turned. 'And don't worry about her mother. I'll be seeing her again in a day or so and then I can reassure her.'

Francesca saw him to the door and wished him a polite goodnight. If it hadn't been imperative that she should see to Peggy at once, she would have gone somewhere quiet and had a good cry. She wasn't sure why she wanted to do this and there really wasn't time to think about it.

Peggy slept all night and Francesca was up and dressed and giving the little girl a drink of lemonade when the professor arrived. He was in flannels and a thick sweater and he hadn't shaved, and she said at once, 'You've been up all night.'

'Not quite all of it. How is Peggy?'

They went to look at her together and he pronounced himself content with her progress. There were more spots now, of course, but her temperature was down a little and she greeted him cheerfully enough. 'Anything in moderation if she's hungry,' he told Francesca, 'and get the elixir started as soon as you can.'

'Thank you for coming. Lucy's made tea—we haven't had our breakfast yet. You'll have a cup?'

He refused pleasantly. 'I must get home and shower and change; I've an out-patients clinic at ten o'clock.'

She opened the door onto a chilly morning.

'I'll look in some time this evening.' He was gone with a casual nod.

It was late in the afternoon when Francesca had a phone call from Peggy's grandmother in Wiltshire. It was a nice, motherly voice with no hint of fussing. 'Renier telephoned. Poor little Peggy, but we are so glad to know that she is being so well looked after. I suppose you haven't heard from her mother?'

'Well, no, the professor said that he would be seeing her and that there was no need to let her know. Peggy is feeling much better and he is looking after her so well, so please don't be anxious.'

'She's our only grandchild and so like our son. He was Renier's friend, you know. They were at university together and school

80

together—he was best man at their wedding and is godfather to Peggy.'

'Would you like to speak to Peggy? She's awake. I'll carry her across to the other bedroom; there's a phone there...'

'That would be delightful. Shall I ring off or wait?'

'If you would wait—I'll be very quick...'

The conversation went on for some time, with Peggy on Francesca's lap, talking non-stop and getting too excited. Presently Francesca whispered, 'Look, Peggy, ask Granny if you can telephone her each day about teatime, and if she says "yes" say goodbye now.'

A satisfactory arrangement for all parties.

The professor came in the evening, once more the epitome of the well-dressed gentleman. He was coolly polite to Francesca, spent ten minutes with Peggy, who was tired and a little peevish now, pronounced himself satisfied and, after only the briefest of conversations, went away again.

'No need to come in the morning,' he observed, 'but I'll take a look about this time tomorrow.'

The next day he told Francesca that Peggy might get up in her dressing-gown and roam the house. 'Keep her warm, she needs a week or so before she goes back to school. You're dealing with the spots, aren't you? She mustn't scratch.'

The next day he told her that he would be seeing Eloise on the following day.

'How nice,' said Francesca tartly. 'I'm sure you will be able to reassure her. Peggy's granny has been phoning each afternoon; she sounds just like a granny ...' A silly remark, she realised, but she went on, 'Peggy's very fond of her.'

'Yes, I know. I shall do my best to persuade Eloise to let her go and stay with her for a few days. You will have to go too, of course.'

'But what about Lucy?'

'I imagine that it could be arranged for her to board for a week or so? Eloise will pay, of course. Would Lucy mind?'

'I think she would love it ... but it will be quite an expense.'

'Not for Eloise, and Peggy will need someone with her.'

'What about Tom?'

'I'm sure that her grandmother will make him welcome. I'll let you know.'

He made his usual abrupt departure.

'Most unsatisfactory,' said Francesca to the empty room. She told Lucy, of course, who found it a marvellous idea. 'They have such fun, the boarders—and almost all of my friends are boarders. Do you suppose Mrs Vincent will pay for me?'

'Professor Pitt-Colwyn seemed to think she would. He's going to let me know...'

'Well, of course,' said Lucy airily. 'If they're

in love they'll do anything to please each other. I bet you anything that he'll be back in a few days with everything arranged.'

She was right. Several days later he arrived at teatime, just as they were sitting on the floor in front of the fire, toasting crumpets.

Peggy, no longer spotty but decidedly pasty-faced, rushed to meet him.

'Where have you been? I missed you. Francesca and Lucy missed you too.'

He picked her up and kissed her. 'Well, now I'm here, may I have a cup of tea and one of those crumpets? There's a parcel in the hall for you, too.' He put her down. 'Run and get it; it's from your mother.'

'Will you have a cup of tea?' asked Francesca in a hostess voice and, at his mocking smile and nod, went on, 'Peggy seems to be quite well again, no temperature for three days, but she's so pale...'

She came into the room then with the parcel and began to unwrap it without much enthusiasm. A doll—a magnificent creature, elaborately dressed.

'How very beautiful,' said Francesca. 'You must give her a name. What a lovely present from Mummy.'

'She's like all my other dolls and I don't like any of them. I like my teddy and Tom.' Peggy put the doll carefully on a chair and climbed on to the professor's lap. 'I had a crumpet,' she told him, 'but I can have some of yours, can't I?'

'Provided you don't drip butter all over me and Francesca allows it.'

Francesca passed a large paper serviette over without a word, and poured the fresh tea Lucy had made. That young lady settled herself on the rug before the fire once again and sank her teeth into a crumpet.

'Do tell,' she said. 'Is—?' She caught the professor's eye. 'Oh, yes, of course,' and went on airily, 'did you have a nice time wherever you went?'

The professor, who had spent exactly twenty-four hours in Birmingham—a city he disliked—only four of which had been in Eloise's company, replied blandly that indeed he had had a most interesting time, as he had a flying visit to Edinburgh and, since heart transplants had often to be dealt with at the most awkward of hours, an all-night session there and, upon his return, another operation in the early hours of the morning at Regent's. Francesca, unaware of this, of course, allowed her imagination to run riot.

She said waspishly, 'I expect a man in your position can take a holiday more or less when he likes. Have another crumpet?'

He took one and allowed Peggy to bite from it before demolishing it.

'There are no more crumpets, I'm afraid,' said Francesca coldly, 'but there is plenty of bread. I can make toast...'

He was sitting back with his eyes closed. 'Delicious—well buttered and spread with Marmite. You know the way to a man's heart, Francesca.'

He opened one eye and smiled at her, but she pretended not to see that and went away to fetch some bread and a pot of Marmite. She put the kettle on again too, foreseeing yet another pot of tea.

The other three were talking about Christmas and laughing a great deal when she got back, and it wasn't until he had at last eaten everything he had been offered that he exchanged a glance with Lucy, who got up at once. 'Peggy! Help me take everything into the kitchen, will you, and we'll wash up? You can have an apron and do the washing; I'll dry.'

Peggy scrambled off the professor's knee. 'You'll not go away?'

'No. What is more, if I'm allowed to, I'll stay until you're in your bed.'

Left alone with him, Francesca cast around in her head for a suitable topic of conversation and came up with, 'Did Mrs Vincent give you any messages for me?'

'None. She thinks it a splendid idea that Peggy should go to her grandmother's for a week or so and that you will go with her. She is quite willing to pay for Lucy to stay at school during that time since she is inconveniencing you. She has asked me to make the arrangements and deal with the travelling and payment of bills and so forth. Oh, and she wishes Mrs Wells to come each day as usual while you're away.'

'Tom Kitten ...?'

'He can surely go with you; I can't imagine that Peggy will go without him.'

'No. I'm sure she wouldn't. You reassured Mrs Vincent about Peggy not being well? She's not worried?'

The professor had a brief memory of Eloise's pretty face turning petulant at the threat of her new, exciting life being disrupted. 'No,' he said quietly. 'She is content to leave Peggy in your charge.'

'When are we to go?'

'Sunday morning. That gives you three days in which to pack and leave everything as you would wish it here. I'll telephone Mrs Vincent and talk to her about it; I know that she will be delighted.'

'It won't be too much work for her?'

'She and Mr Vincent have plenty of help. Besides, they love Peggy.'

'Am I to ask Lucy's headmistress if she can board for a week or two?'

'I'll attend to that as well.'

Lucy and Peggy came back then. 'I've washed up,' piped Peggy importantly, 'and now I'm going to have a bath and go to bed. I'll be so very very quick and if you like you can see where my spots were.'

'I look forward to that,' he assured her

gravely. 'In ten minutes' time.'

He went as soon as Peggy, bathed and in her nightgown, had solemnly shown him the faint scars from her spots and then bidden him a sleepy goodnight.

His goodbyes were brief, with the remark that he would telephone some time on Saturday to make final arrangements for Sunday.

Lucy was over the moon; she was popular at school and had many friends and, although she had never said so, Francesca was aware that she would like to have been a boarder, and, as for Peggy, when she was told there was no containing her excitement. Something of their pleasure rubbed off on to Francesca and she found herself looking forward to the visit. The future seemed uncertain: there was still no word from Mrs Vincent, although Peggy had had a postcard from Carlisle. There had been no message on it, merely a scrawled, 'Hope you are being a good girl, love Mummy.'

Francesca's efforts to get Peggy to make a crayon drawing for her mother or buy a postcard to send to her came to nought. She wrote to Mrs Vincent's solicitor, enclosing a letter to her and asking him to forward it. She gave a faithful account of Peggy's progress and enclosed an accurate rendering of the money she had spent from the housekeeping allowance, assured her that the little girl was quite well again and asked her to let her know if

87

there was anything special she wished done. The solicitor replied immediately; he understood from Mrs Vincent that it was most unlikely that she would be returning home for some time and Miss Haley was to do whatever she thought was best for Peggy. It wasn't very satisfactory, but Francesca realised that she would have to make the best of it. At least she could call upon the professor again if anything went wrong, and, now that they were going to stay with Peggy's grandparents for a while, they would surely accept responsibility for the child.

The professor telephoned quite early on Saturday morning; he would take Lucy to her school and at the same time have a word with the headmistress. 'Just to make sure that everything is in order,' he explained in what Francesca described to herself as his soothing voice.

'Should I go with you?' she wanted to know.

'No need. I dare say you've already had a few words with her.'

Francesca, feeling guilty, said that yes, she had. 'Just about her clothes and so on,' she said placatingly, and was answered by a mocking grunt.

He arrived on the doorstep in the afternoon with Brontes sitting on the back seat, greeted her with casual civility, assured Peggy that he would take her to her granny's in the morning, waited while Lucy bade Francesca goodbye at some length and then drove her away, refusing politely to return for tea. 'I'm expecting a call from Eloise,' he explained, watching Francesca's face.

Lucy telephoned in the evening; she sounded happy and any doubts that Francesca might have had about her sister's feeling homesick were swept away. She promised to phone herself when they arrived at Peggy's grandparents' house and went away to finish packing.

The professor arrived in time for coffee which Mrs Wells, who had popped round to take the keys and lock up, had ready. He was in an affable mood, answering Peggy's questions with patience while Brontes brooded in a kindly fashion over Tom. Francesca drank her coffee and had nothing to say, conscious that just having the professor there was all she wanted; he annoyed her excessively at times and she didn't think that he liked her overmuch but, all the same, when he was around she felt that there was no need for her to worry about anything. The future was vague—once Mrs Vincent came home she would be out of work again—but then in the meantime she was saving almost every penny of her wages and she liked her job. Moreover, she had become very fond of Peggy.

Rather to her surprise, she was told to sit in the front of the car. 'Brontes will take care of Peggy,' said the professor. 'Tom can sit in the middle in his basket.'

She stayed prudently silent until they joined the M4 where he put a large, well-shod foot down and allowed the car to slide past everything else in the fast lane. 'Just where are we going?' she asked a shade tartly.

'Oh, dear, did I not tell you? But you do know Wiltshire?' When she nodded he added, 'Just on the other side of the Berkshire border. Marlborough is the nearest town. The village is called Nether Tawscombe. They live in the Old Rectory, a charming old place.'

'You've been there before?'

He laughed shortly. 'I spent a number of school holidays there with Jeff and later, when we were at Cambridge and medical school, we spent a good deal of time there.'

'Then he got married,' prompted Francesca.

'Yes. Eloise was never happy there; she dislikes the country.'

Something in his voice stopped her from saying anything more; she turned round to see how the occupants of the back seat were getting on. Peggy had an arm round Brontes's great neck, she had stuck the fingers of her other hand through the mesh in front of Tom's basket and wore an expression of happiness which turned her plain little face into near prettiness. Francesca, who had had secret doubts about the visit, knew that she had been mistaken.

They arrived at Nether Tawscombe in time

for lunch. The one village street was empty under the thin, wintry sunshine, but the houses which lined it looked charming. They got larger as the street went uphill until it reached the church, surrounded by a churchyard and ringed around by fair-sized houses. The Old Rectory was close by; an open gate led to a low, rambling house with diamond-paned windows and a solid front door.

As the professor stopped before it, it was opened and an elderly man came to meet them. She stood a little on one side until Peggy's excited greetings were over and the two men had shaken hands. She was led indoors while the professor saw to their baggage. The hall was stone-flagged, long and narrow, with a door opening on to the garden at the back of the house at its end. Brontes had made straight for it and had been joined by a black Labrador, who had rushed out of an open doorway as a grey-haired lady, cosily plump, had come into the hall.

Peggy screamed with delight and flung herself at her grandmother, and Mr Vincent said to Francesca, 'Always had a soft spot for each other—haven't had her to stay for a long time. This is delightful, Miss—er ...?'

'Would you call me Francesca, please? Peggy does.'

Mrs Vincent came to take her hand then, with a warmth which caused sudden tears to prick her eyelids; for the last few years she had been without that kindly warmth...

That the professor was an old friend and welcome guest was evident: he hugged Mrs Vincent, asked which rooms the bags were to go to, and went up the wide staircase with the air of a man who knew his way about blindfold.

Mrs Vincent saw Francesca's eyes follow him and said comfortably, 'We've known Renier for many years. He and our son were friends; he spent many a school holiday here and Jeff went over to Holland. He's a good man, but I suspect you've discovered that for yourself, Miss ... may I call you Francesca?'

'Oh, yes, please. What would you like me to do? Take Peggy upstairs and tidy her for lunch? She's so happy and excited.'

'Yes, dear. You do exactly what you've been doing. We know so little about her day-to-day life now that her father is dead—he brought her here very often, you see.'

No mention of Eloise, reflected Francesca. It wasn't her business, of course. She bore Peggy away upstairs to a couple of low-ceilinged rooms with a communicating door and windows overlooking the wintry garden beyond. After London, even the elegant part of London, it was sheer bliss.

The professor stayed to lunch and she was mystified to hear him say that no, he wasn't going back to London.

'Having a quiet weekend at Pomfritt Cleeve?

Splendid,' observed Mr Vincent, and most annoyingly said no more about it.

Renier took his leave soon after lunch, saying goodbye to Francesca last of all, patting her shoulder in an avuncular fashion and remarking casually that he would probably see her at some time. She stood in the hall with everyone else, wishing with all her heart that she were going with him. For that was where she wanted to be, she realised with breath-taking surprise, with him all the time, forever and ever, and, now she came to think about it, she had been in love with him for quite some time, only she had never allowed herself to think about it. Now he was going; not that that would make any difference—he had always treated her at best with friendliness, more often than not with an uninterested politeness. She looked away so that she didn't see him go through the door.

However sad the state of her heart, she had little time to brood over it. Peggy was a different child, behaving like any normal six-year-old would behave, playing endless games with the Labrador and Tom, racing around the large garden with Francesca in laughing pursuit, going for rides on the elderly donkey who lived in the paddock behind the house, going to the shops in Marlborough with her grandmother and Francesca. She had quickly acquired a splendid appetite and slept the moment her small head touched the pillow. A good thing too, thought Francesca, for by bedtime she was tired herself. She loved her days in the quiet village and Mr and Mrs Vincent treated her like a daughter. Sometimes she felt guilty that she should be living so comfortably while Lucy was in London, although she thought that her sister, from all accounts, was as happy as she was herself. They missed each other, but Francesca had the sense to see that it was good for Lucy to learn independence. She tried not to think of the professor too often and she felt that she was succeeding, until after a week or so Lucy wrote her usual letter and mentioned that he had been to see her at the school and had taken her out to tea. 'To the Ritz, no less!' scrawled Lucy, with a lot of exclamation marks.

The professor, having returned Lucy to her school, went to his home and sat down in his great chair by the fire with Brontes pressed against his knee and mother cat and the kittens asleep in their basket to keep him company. Tea with Lucy had been rewarding and he had made no bones about asking questions, although he had put them in such a way that she hadn't been aware of how much she was telling him. Indeed, she had confided in him that her headmistress had offered her a place in a group of girls from her class going to Switzerland for a skiing holiday. 'But of course I can't go,' she had told him. 'It's a lot of money and Fran couldn't possibly afford it—I mean, we both have to have new winter coats, and if Mrs Vincent comes back we'll have to move again, won't we?'

He had agreed with her gravely, at the same time prising out as much information about the trip as he could. He stroked Brontes's great head. 'I shall have to pay another visit to Eloise,' he told the dog. 'Now how can I fit that in next week?'

Presently he picked up the telephone on the table beside him and dialled a number.

A week, ten days went by. Peggy was so happy that Francesca began to worry about their return; she saw that the child loved her grandparents and they in turn loved her. They didn't spoil her, but she was treated with a real affection which Francesca felt she had never had from her mother. One morning when Peggy had gone off with her grandfather, leaving Francesca to catch up on the washing and ironing of the child's wardrobe, Mrs Vincent came to sit with her in the little room behind the kitchen where the ironing was done. 'You must be wondering why we don't mention Peggy's mother. Oh, I know we talk about her because Peggy must not forget her mother, but you see Eloise never wanted her and when she was born she turned against her—you see she takes after my son, and Eloise was so pretty. She said that her friends would laugh at such an ugly child. It upset Jeff, but she was fortunate—he was a loyal husband; he took Peggy around with him as much as possible and they adored each other. It was a pity that Peggy overheard her mother telling someone one day that she wished the child had not been born. She never told her father, bless the child, but she did tell Mrs Wells, who told me. There is nothing I would like better than to have Peggy to live with us always.'

'Have you suggested it to Eloise?'

'No; you see she will probably marry again and he might like to have Peggy for a daughter.'

Francesca thought Mrs Vincent was talking about the professor. She said woodenly, 'Yes, I dare say that would be very likely.'

It seemed as though it might be true, for the very next day he arrived just as they were sitting down to lunch.

Francesca, going out to the kitchen to ask Bertha, the housekeeper, if she could grill another few chops for their unexpected guest, was glad of her errand: it gave her time to assume the politely cool manner she could hide behind. It was difficult to maintain it, though, for when she got back to the dining-room it was to hear him telling the Vincents that he was on his way to see Eloise. 'I shall be glad of a word with you, sir,' he told Mr Vincent, 'as my visit concerns Peggy, and I think you should know why I am going.'

Francesca ate her chop—sawdust and ashes in her mouth. Afterwards she couldn't remember eating it; nor could she remember what part she took in the conversation during the meal. It must have been normal, for no one looked at her in surprise. She couldn't wait for the professor to be gone, and as though he knew that he sat over coffee, teasing Peggy and having a perfectly unnecessary conversation with Mrs Vincent about the uses of the old-fashioned remedies she used for minor ailments.

He got up at length and went away with Mr Vincent to the study, to emerge half an hour later and, amid a great chorus of goodbyes, take his leave.

This time Francesca watched him go; when next she saw him he would most likely be engaged to Eloise—even married. She was vague about special licences but, the professor being the man he was, she had no doubt that if he wished to procure one at a moment's notice he would find a way to do so.

It was three days later when Mr Vincent remarked to his wife, 'Renier phoned. He has got his way. He's back in London, but too busy to come down and see us for a few days.'

Mrs Vincent beamed. 'Tell me later—how delightful; he must be very happy.' Francesca, making a Plasticine cat for Peggy, did her best to feel happy, because he was happy, and one should be glad to know that someone one loved was happy, shouldn't one? She found it hard work.

He came at the end of the week, walking in unannounced during a wet afternoon. He looked tired; he worked too hard, thought Francesca lovingly, scanning the weary lines on his handsome face. He also looked smug—something she found hard to understand.

CHAPTER FIVE

Renier had had lunch, he assured Mrs Vincent, before going with Mr Vincent to the study again. When they came back into the sitting-room the older man said, 'Well, my dear, it's all settled. Which of us shall tell Peggy?'

'What?' asked Peggy, all ears. 'Is—is it something nice? Like I can stay here forever?'

'You clever girl to guess,' said Mrs Vincent, and gave her a hug. 'That's exactly what you are going to do—live here with Grandpa and me and go to school every day.'

Peggy flung herself at her grandfather. 'Really, truly? I may stay here with you? I won't have to go back to Mummy? She doesn't want me, you know.'

'Well, darling, your mummy is a very busy person and being on stage is very hard work. You can go and see her whenever you want to,' said Mrs Vincent.

'Shan't want to. Where will Francesca go?'

Francesca went on fixing a tail to another cat

and didn't look up. 'If there is no objection, I think it might be a good idea if I took her somewhere quiet and explained everything to her,' said the professor.

He added gently, 'Get your coat, Francesca, and come with me.'

'Now that is a good idea,' said Mrs Vincent. 'Run along, dear; Renier will explain everything to you so much better than we can.'

There was no point in refusing; she fetched her old Burberry and went out to the car with him, to be greeted with pleasure by Brontes, who was roaming the garden. The professor opened the door and stuffed her gently into her seat, got in beside her and, with Brontes's great head wedged between their shoulders, drove off.

'Where am I going?' asked Francesca coldly.

'Pomfritt Cleeve. I have a cottage there. We can talk quietly.'

'What about? Surely you could have told me at Mrs Vincent's house?'

'No, this concerns you as well as Peggy.'

He had turned off the main road into a narrow, high-hedged lane going downhill, and presently she saw a cluster of lights through the gathering dusk. A minute or so later they had reached the village—one street with a church halfway along, a shop or two, and small, old cottages, well maintained—before he turned into another narrow lane, and after a hundred yards or so drove through a propped-open gate and stopped before a thatched cottage of some size. There were lights in the windows and the door was thrown open as she got out of the car, hesitating for a moment, giving Brontes time to rush through the door with a delighted bark, almost knocking down the stout little lady standing there. She said, 'Good doggie,' in a soft, West Country voice and then added, 'come on in out of the cold, sir, and the young lady. There's a good fire in the sitting-room and tea in ten minutes.'

The professor flung an arm around her cosy person and kissed her soundly. 'Blossom, how very nice to see you again—and something smells delicious.'

He caught Francesca gently by the arm. 'Francesca, this is Blossom, who lives here and looks after the cottage for me. Blossom, this is Miss Haley. Take her away so that she can tidy herself if she wants to, and we'll have tea in ten minutes, just as you say.'

The cottage, decided Francesca, wasn't a cottage really. It might look like one, but it was far too big to warrant such a name, although there was nothing grand about it. The sitting-room to which she was presently shown was low-ceilinged with comfortable chairs and tables dotted around on the polished floor. There was a low table before the fire and sofas on either side of it. She sat opposite her host, pouring tea into delicate china cups and eating scones warm from the oven and, having been well brought up, made light conversation.

However, not for long. 'Let us dispense with the small talk,' said the professor, 'and get down to facts. Eloise is quite happy to allow Peggy to live with her grandparents. She will of course be free to see the child whenever she wishes, but she will remarry very shortly and intends to stay on the stage, so it isn't likely that she will visit Peggy more than once in a while. Mrs Vincent will employ her old nanny's daughter to look after Peggy, so you may expect to leave as soon as she arrives.' Francesca gave a gasp, but he went on, 'Don't interrupt, I have not yet finished. Lucy has been told that she may join a school party going to Switzerland to ski—I have seen her headmistress and she will join the party.'

'Now look here,' said Francesca, and was hushed once more.

'I haven't said anything to you, for I knew that you would refuse to do anything about it. The child deserves a holiday and, as for the costs, you can repay me when you are able.'

'But I haven't got a job,' said Francesca wildly. 'I never heard such arrogance—going behind my back and making plans and arranging things—'

'Ah, yes, as to arrangements for yourself, Eloise is quite agreeable to your remaining at the cottage for a few days so that you can pack your things.'

She goggled at him, bereft of words. That

she loved him dearly went without saying, but at the moment she wished for something solid to throw at him. 'You have been busy, haven't you?' she said nastily.

'Yes, indeed I have. I shall drive Lucy over to Zeebrugge to meet the school party there; you would like to come with us, no doubt.'

'How can I? I'll have to look for a job—'

'Well, as to that, I have a proposal to make.' He was sitting back, watching her, smiling faintly.

'Well, I don't want to hear it,' she declared roundly. 'I shan't listen to anything more you may say—'

'Perhaps this isn't the right time, after all. You are cross, are you not? But there is really nothing you can do about it, is there? You will break young Lucy's heart if you refuse to let her go to Switzerland—'

'She had no skiing clothes.'

'Now she has all she needs—a Christmas present.'

She all but ground her teeth. 'And I suppose you're going to get married?'

'That is my intention.'

Rage and despair almost choked her, and she allowed rage to take over.

'I hope you will be very happy.' Her voice was icy and not quite steady.

'I am certain of that.'

'I'd like to go back.' He agreed at once, which was a good thing—otherwise she might have burst into tears. Where was she to go? And there was Lucy to think of when she got back from Switzerland. Would she have time to get a job by then? And would her small hoard of money be sufficient to keep them until she had found work again? There were so many questions to be answered. Perhaps she should have listened to this proposal he had mentioned—it could have been another job—but pride wouldn't allow her to utter another word. She bade Blossom goodbye, complimented her on her scones and got into the car; it smelled comfortingly of leather and, very faintly, of Brontes.

Strangely enough, the great bulk of the professor beside her was comforting too, although she could think of no good reason why it should be.

Back at the Vincents' house after a silent drive, he bade them goodbye, bent his great height to Peggy's hug, observed cheerfully to Francesca that he would be in touch, and left.

She had no idea what he had said to the Vincents, but from what they said she gathered that they understood her to have a settled future, and there seemed no point in enlightening them. Peggy, chattering excitedly as Francesca put her to bed, seemed to think that she would see her as often as she wanted, and Francesca said nothing to disillusion her. The future was her own problem.

She left the Vincents' two days later, and was

driven back to the mews cottage by Mr Vincent. She hated leaving the quiet village. Moreover, she had grown very fond of Peggy who, even while bidding her a tearful goodbye, was full of plans to see her again, which were seconded by her grandmother. She had responded suitably and kept up a cheerful conversation with her companion as they drove but, once he had left her at the empty house, with the observation that they would be seeing each other shortly, she sat down in the kitchen and had a good cry. She felt better after that, made a cup of tea, and unpacked before starting on the task of repacking Lucy's cases as well as her own. There had been a brief letter for her before she left the Vincents', telling her that they would be crossing over to Zeebrugge in two days' time, and would she be ready to leave by nine o'clock in the morning and not a minute later?

Mrs Wells had kept the place spotless, and there was a note on the kitchen table saying that she would come in the morning; there was a little ironing and nothing else to do but pack. She was halfway through that when Lucy phoned.

'You're back. Isn't it exciting? I can't believe it's true. I'm coming home tomorrow afternoon. The bus leaves here in the evening, but Renier says he'll take us to Zeebrugge early the next day and I can join the others there. Isn't he a darling?' She didn't wait for

Francesca's answer, which was just as well. 'Oh, Fran, I do love being a boarder. I know I can't be, but you have no idea what fun it is. I've been asked to lots of parties at Christmas, too.'

Francesca let her talk. There was time enough to worry over the problem of Christmas; she still had almost three weeks to find a job and somewhere for them to live, too.

'You're very quiet,' said Lucy suddenly.

'I've had a busy day; I'm packing for us both now—I'll do the rest tomorrow. I've got to talk to Mrs Wells, too.'

'I'll help you. You are looking forward to the trip, aren't you?'

'Tremendously,' said Francesca with her fingers crossed. 'See you tomorrow, Lucy.'

By the time Lucy arrived, she had done everything that was necessary. Mrs Wells had been more than helpful, arranging to come early in the morning to take the keys and lock up. The solicitor had been dealt with, she had been to the bank and taken out as much money as she dared, found their passports—unused since they had been on holiday in France with their parents—and, finally, written a letter to Mrs Vincent which she had enclosed in a letter to the solicitor. There was nothing more to do but have a good gossip and go to bed.

The Bentley purred to a halt outside the cottage at precisely nine o'clock, then the professor got out, wished them an affable good-morning, put Francesca's overnight bag and Lucy's case in the boot, enquired as to what had been done with the rest of their luggage—safely with Mrs Wells—and urged them to get in. 'You go in front, Lucy,' said Francesca and nipped into the back seat, not seeing his smile, and resolutely looked out of the window all the way to Dover, trying not to listen to the cheerful talk between the other two.

Five hours later they were in Zeebrugge, driving to the hotel where the rest of the party had spent the night, and it was only then that she realised that she had no idea what was to happen next. There wasn't any time to think about it; the bus was ready to leave. It was only after a hasty goodbye to Lucy, when she was watching the party drive away, that the full awkwardness of the situation dawned upon her. 'Whatever am I going to do?' She had turned on the professor, her voice shrill with sudden fright. 'When is there a boat back?'

He took her arm. 'We are going to my home in Holland for the night. My mother will be delighted to meet you.'

'I must get back—I have to find a job.'

He took no notice, merely urged her gently into the car, got in beside her and drove off.

'This is ridiculous ... I've been a fool—I thought we would be going straight back. I'm to spend the night at Mrs Wells's house.'

'We will telephone her.' His voice was

soothing as well as matter-of-fact. 'We shall soon be home.'

They were already through Brugge and on the motorway, bypassing Antwerp, crossing into Holland, and racing up the Dutch motorways to Tilburg, Nijmegen and on past Arnhem. The wintry afternoon was turning to an early dusk and, save for a brief halt for coffee and sandwiches, they hadn't stopped. Francesca, trying to make sense of the situation, sat silent, her mind addled with tiredness and worry and a deep-seated misery, because once they were back in England there would be no reason to see the professor ever again. The thought cast her in such deep gloom that she barely noticed the country had changed; the road ran through trees and thick shrubbery with a light glimpsed here and there. The professor turned off the road through a gateway, slowed along a narrow, sanded drive and stopped before the house at its end. He leaned over, undid her safety belt, got out and helped her out too, and she stood for a moment, looking at the dark bulk of the house. It was square and solid, its big windows lighted, frost sparkling on the iron balcony above the porch.

She said in a forlorn voice, 'I should never have come with you. I should never have let you take over my life, and Lucy's, too. I'm very grateful for your help; you have been kind and I expect it suited you and Eloise. I can't think why you've brought me here.'

'You wouldn't listen to my proposal at Pomfritt Cleeve,' the professor had come very close, 'I can see that I shall have to try again.' He put his arms around her and held her very close. 'You are a stubborn, proud girl with a beautiful head full of muddled thoughts, and I love you to distraction. I fell in love with you the first time I saw you, and what is all this nonsense about Eloise? I don't even like the woman, but something had to be done about Peggy. Now you will listen, my darling, while I make you a proposal. Will you marry me?'

What with his great arms around her and her heart thumping against her ribs, Francesca hadn't much breath—only just enough to say, 'Yes, oh, yes, Renier,' before he bent to kiss her.

THE ENGAGEMENT

CHAPTER ONE

'Gotcha!'

Kristin Mabry snatched Watson by the throat, then began the seemingly endless task of uncoiling him from the leg of a chair. Watson was a snake—a six-foot boa constrictor, to be precise—part of the extensive collection of animals acquired by Kristin's eight-year-old son, Randy. The collection included two brown mice named Agatha and Christie, a parakeet named Hercule Poirot, Sherlock the sheepdog and Holmes the cat. Kristin's son was a fan of the mystery novel.

After finally extracting Watson from beneath the chair, Kristin was rewarded by a rather startling hiss. 'Well,' she said. 'Back in the cage with you.'

Having placed Watson in his terrarium, replete with tree limb and pond, Kristin plopped down on the sofa and swung her feet up. Then she glanced over at the cat, who crouched on the chair next to her. Holmes was a superb listener, and at the moment Kristin Mabry needed a listener badly.

'I'm having one of those days, Holmes. Ever since I got up this morning, nothing in my life seems quite right.' Kristin gazed at Holmes. Holmes gazed back, golden-green eyes thoughtful and sagacious. Holmes was a truly beautiful cat, with a glossy calico coat stippled in russet and brown. Kristin's son had rescued him at kittenhood, when he'd been a scrawny little snippet of fur abandoned at the door of the veterinary clinic in Denver run by Kristin and her husband. Ex-husband now, of course.

'Sometimes I wonder,' Kristin went on quickly. 'Did I make the right decision, after all? Moving here to Oklahoma, uprooting Randy the way I did ... I suppose all mothers worry, but the truth is, Randy's been too quiet these past few weeks. He almost wouldn't go to swimming class today—just wanted to hide out in his room. That's not like him. Usually he's charging in all directions at once.'

Holmes blinked slowly, wisely. Kristin sighed.

'You're lucky, Holmes. You're a cat. Your only problems are avoiding Sherlock and annoying Agatha and Christie. I have to admit sometimes I envy you. No real worries. No betrayal from the one person you thought you could trust—'

A slight noise interrupted Kristin, and she glanced up to find a man standing on her porch, looking in at her through the screen door. She felt mortified. How long had the man been standing there, listening as she spilled out her most private concerns? Spilled them out to her cat, on top of everything else. Mustering as much dignity as possible in her cutoffs and faded T-shirt, she stood and crossed to the

112

door.

'May I help you?' she said stiffly.

'That depends.' The man had a deep, leisurely voice, and an easy grin. 'I hate to interrupt your therapy session with your cat.'

Kristin flushed, imagining the spectacle she'd provided, stretched out on her couch, Holmes sitting in the chair beside her—the picture of patient and therapist. Since her divorce she'd confided in Holmes a great deal, an embarrassing habit she preferred no one to know about.

Now Kristin studied the man through the screen door. He was tall, dark-haired, completely unfamiliar to her. But after only two weeks in town, just about everyone in Danfield was unfamiliar to her.

'There's a perfectly logical explanation for what I was doing,' she said. 'It helps to talk about your problems out loud, you know. Makes them seem manageable.'

'Hmm ... manageable. Of course.' The man was obviously amused. Kristin felt obliged to elaborate further, even though she suspected she was only making matters worse.

'Holmes is a lot cheaper than a psychiatrist,' she said, deadpan. 'Besides, his advice has never once steered me wrong.'

This appeared to give the man something to think about.

'At least your cat's reliable,' he said. 'Nothing worse than a pet who gives bad

113

advice.'

Kristin laughed. 'May I help you?' she asked again.

The man surveyed her quizzically through the screen door. 'I'm looking for the new vet, Kristin Mabry. *Dr.* Kristin Mabry.'

Kristin knew that at the moment she didn't look like a veterinarian, not in her cutoffs, her blond hair draggling in this humid summer weather, her feet bare. Nonetheless, she opened the screen door and strode onto the porch in a professional manner.

'I'm Dr. Mabry,' she said.

'Andrew O'Donnell.' He reached out to shake her hand, his grip cool and firm. With the screen no longer between them, she gave him another glance. He had strong features, his hair the color of charcoal, his eyes a dark gray—definitely an attractive man. Since her divorce, Kristin had made a point not to notice whether a man was handsome or not. Why was she paying attention now?

Andrew O'Donnell wore a casual denim shirt, the pockets bristling with an assortment of pens and pencils. His tie was boldly patterned and managed to convey a certain nonchalance—loosely knotted at his neck, the ends hanging at reckless, uneven angles. He also wore slim black jeans and cowboy boots. Kristin drew her eyebrows together. Unfortunately, there was something appealing about a man in black jeans and cowboy

114

boots...

'Mr. O'Donnell, *may* I help you?' she asked again.

'I'm your volunteer, Dr. Mabry.'

'Volunteer? I'm afraid I don't understand.'

'Could've sworn you were the one.' He rooted through a shirt pocket and produced an impressive collection of business cards. With practiced ease he flipped rapidly through them, scanning a note jotted on the back of one card. 'Yes. Says so right here. A volunteer for Dr. Kristin Mabry.' Andrew glanced at her, his expression ironic this time. 'I'm your man, Dr. Mabry. I'm your son's new dad.'

Kristin shook her head skeptically. Last week she'd learned that the Danfield Community Center recruited local businessmen to spend time with fatherless children. The Substitute Dad program, it was called. For all intents and purposes, Kristin's eight-year-old son Randy was fatherless now, and she'd immediately signed up for the program. Randy needed to have a man around, a male role model. Since Kristin didn't plan to date any time soon—maybe not for another century or so—she knew she had to be innovative in finding that role model for her son.

'Mr. O'Donnell, it's true my son needs a substitute dad. But I was told I'd be screening the files of all the applicants, and then there'd be a lengthy period of interviews and background checks.'

Andrew tucked the business cards back into his pocket; it was a wonder they all fit. He began to look a bit disgruntled. 'I guess I haven't explained the situation clearly enough, Dr. Mabry. I've been assigned to work with your son—no choice in the matter. It's a court order.'

Kristin shook her head again. 'Now I really don't understand.'

'Just consider me a convenience.' Andrew's tone was sardonic. 'The legal system in Danfield has taken care of everything for you. I'm your son's volunteer dad—signed, sealed and delivered.'

Kristin gave this man—this handsome Andrew O'Donnell—a thoughtful frown. 'Nonsense,' she said. 'I want my son to have the best experience possible with the program. I was assured I'd be able to choose among several applicants.'

'You didn't count on the Honorable Loraine Thaxter.' Now Andrew sounded grim. 'Loraine is the judge who slapped me with this injunction. I've been assigned to forty hours of community service with your son. End of story.'

'No. I think you're just at the beginning of your story, Mr. O'Donnell. I find this whole thing very peculiar, and I want to know exactly what's going on here.'

Andrew O'Donnell paced the small porch as

if eager to leave. 'You don't need to hear all the circumstances. I've been assigned to do a job and I'll do it. No getting out of it. I've already tried that, and it didn't work.'

'How reassuring,' Kristin said. 'An unwilling volunteer father.'

Andrew gave her a distracted glance. 'Look, Dr. Mabry, I have nothing against kids. Kids are fine. But this isn't the best of times for me to get involved. I'm trying to pull off an important business deal.'

'Business deal. I see.' Andrew O'Donnell didn't look like a typical executive. 'What is it you do for a living?' she asked.

'I own a company that makes watches—timepieces, actually. Hand-tooled, the way my great-grandfather used to do it.' He stopped pacing; obviously Kristin had hit on a subject of interest to Andrew O'Donnell. Her gaze strayed to the silver wristwatch he wore. Old-fashioned and elegant, it evoked a sense of agelessness. She wondered if it was one he'd manufactured.

'Watchmaking seems like a respectable vocation,' she said.

He grinned. 'Don't assume I'm respectable. I ran a saloon down in Oklahoma City for years. I've only recently taken over the family business.'

'A saloon ...' Clearly the man wanted to keep her off balance. 'Mr. O'Donnell, about this court order you're under. Apparently you're in some sort of trouble with the law.'

'One thing I can tell you, Dr. Mabry, it's no use fighting the legal system in Danfield. Your son and I are going to be stuck with each other for a while. We'll just have to make the best of it. Why don't you introduce me to your boy, and we'll go from there.'

'Slow down. For one thing, Randy's not around. He's at his swimming class. And I still don't understand what on earth this is all about.' Kristin gestured toward her porch chairs. 'Mr. O'Donnell, have a seat. Please. And tell me what's going on!'

Andrew took time to consider this request. 'Will the cat be joining us?' he asked.

Kristin waited. Finally Andrew O'Donnell moved toward the wicker furniture crammed at one end of the porch.

The lacy, delicate wicker chairs and table had originally graced Kristin's porch in Denver. She'd lived in a perfect house in Denver, a rambling Queen Anne with plenty of nooks and crannies, room for all manner of homey clutter. But here in Oklahoma, Kristin had only been able to afford this boxy little brick house, an uninspired structure with a meager porch added on like an afterthought. The wicker furniture barely fit, and Andrew had to squeeze around the table to get to a seat.

Obviously he wasn't a man suited to wicker. The chair creaked as he shifted his weight, and he seemed to be searching in vain for a comfortable position. Kristin slipped into the chair across from him.

'Start at the beginning, Mr. O'Donnell. Who is this Judge Thaxter, and what business does she have involving my son in a court order?'

'Loraine Thaxter's the law around here,' he said dryly. 'Trust me, you don't want to tangle with Loraine. Some of us have found that out the hard way.'

The man kept being evasive. Kristin propped her elbows on the table and leaned toward him. 'Mr. O'Donnell, Danfield is a very small town, and I'm sure it won't be difficult for me to find Judge Thaxter. She can enlighten me even if *you* won't.'

Andrew took on an injured expression. Kristin had been given a similar look by the Doberman dragged into her clinic yesterday for shots. 'Dr. Mabry, believe me, you don't want to know Loraine Thaxter. That lady gets out of hand.'

'I'm starting to think I do want to know her. I suspect she has all sorts of interesting things to say about you, Mr. O'Donnell.'

He didn't answer for a long while. He just kept shifting around in his chair, giving the impression that any minute he would take Kristin's wicker furniture and pitch it over the side of the porch.

Who *was* this man, anyway? Certainly not the role model Kristin had pictured for her son! If nothing else, she'd imagined a volunteer dad perhaps a little more ... grandfatherly. Yes, that was it. She'd hoped for an older gentleman, maybe someone with a white beard. But there was nothing about Andrew O'Donnell that hinted even remotely of the grandfather type. The man was in his prime, surely no more than thirty-five. He had broad shoulders to go with his height, and those strong features of his bordered on stubborn ...

Why was she noting Andrew's good looks again? It only made her feel restless. A breeze rustled through the grass of the lush, overgrown yard but did nothing to alleviate the heat. Kristin longed for the bracing air of the Colorado Rockies. She still wasn't used to this humid Oklahoma climate. The afternoon seemed to press down on her like a heavy, damp blanket, and she pushed a bedraggled strand of hair away from her cheek.

'Mr. O'Donnell, I could go call the judge right now ...'

'All right, all right,' he grumbled. 'Here's how it happened. I made the mistake of dating Judge Loraine Thaxter. We went out for a couple of months, broke up in the natural order of things—and before I knew it, she hit me with this court order.'

'I suspect you're leaving out a few details,' Kristin remarked.

'Nothing important.'

Kristin was growing more and more impatient with the man. 'Mr. O'Donnell, I'm supposed to believe this muddle is about a lovers' quarrel—'

'No, this muddle's about a technicality. An absurd technicality.' By now Andrew looked perturbed. 'While I was a saloon keeper I began collecting antique firearms, Dr. Mabry. Valuable antique firearms. Loraine knows how much that collection means to me. So, after our breakup, out of the blue, she impounded my collection, hauled me before the bench and told me it was either community service or she'd impound *me*, too. Turns out I don't have all the proper licenses for my firearms—or so Loraine says. It doesn't seem to matter to her that most of the guns don't even function anymore. They're antiques, dammit. Those are the facts, Dr. Mabry. Satisfied?'

Kristin had listened with interest. Andrew O'Donnell collected antique guns, and his love life seemed as volatile as gunpowder. 'So you're obliged to do community service,' she said. 'Wonderful. But I'm afraid you'll have to go serve it somewhere else. You're not the volunteer I want for my son. A gunrunning saloon keeper—'

'Don't forget watchmaker.'

'Very well. You're a gunrunning, saloon-keeping watchmaker with a vengeful judge for an ex-girlfriend. I can't honestly say you're the type of person I want my son to emulate.'

Andrew looked Kristin over disapprovingly, as if he found her unsatisfactory, too.

'Loraine's the one who started the Substitute Dad program. It seems she picked up your file and liked the sound of your case. She agrees your son needs a father, and she thinks I need—Hell, never mind that. The point is, I'm here, ready for civic duty.'

Kristin squeezed out of her chair and glared at Andrew O'Donnell. 'Listen, I don't care what your judge says. I'm not a charity case and neither is Randy. We can find someone who really wants to volunteer. I suggest you and the Honorable Loraine patch up your differences and leave us out of it.'

Andrew looked surprised at her outburst. What had he assumed? That she'd be grateful for any assistance, even begrudging? Randy deserved better than that and so did she. Kristin had learned at least one thing from her painful divorce: she and Randy deserved a good life here in Oklahoma, no matter what they'd left behind in Colorado. Andrew O'Donnell and his honorable girlfriend could just solve their problems some other way!

'Mr. O'Donnell, goodbye,' she said firmly. 'This chat of ours has been very informative. If you want my advice, though, watch out who you date in the future. Stay away from judges, policewomen and anyone else involved with the—'

She broke off as she saw her son come up the street from the community center. Randy walked slowly, hands stuffed into the pockets

122

of his shorts, not noticing that the towel slung over his shoulder was about to fall to the ground. A shock of wet blond hair was plastered to his forehead, and he appeared deep in thought. He'd been too thoughtful lately—that was just the problem.

Randy paused to survey the red Bronco parked in front of the house—Andrew O'Donnell's vehicle, no doubt. Randy gave the Bronco his full consideration, then came along again, taking one deliberate stride after another. When he reached the house, he skirted the porch steps and clambered up onto the wooden railing, instead, being a boy who never took the easy route. His towel finally did fall to the ground as he straddled the porch railing. He examined Andrew O'Donnell soberly. Andrew, in turn, examined Randy with equal soberness. The two of them, man and boy, seemed to be taking each other's measure. It was Randy who spoke first, glancing over at Kristin.

'Hi, Mom. Is this my new dad?'

CHAPTER TWO

Unfortunately, once Kristin's eight-year-old son made up his mind about something, he was relentless. And he immediately made up his mind about Andrew O'Donnell. For some reason, Randy took one look at Andrew and decided he'd found the best volunteer dad there was. During the next few days, no amount of logic could shake Randy's conviction. Kristin checked out Andrew O'Donnell and found him to be reputable, in spite of his romantic problems with the local judge. Then, reluctantly, she gave in. She allowed her persuasive young son to talk her into giving Andrew O'Donnell a run as a substitute father.

On their first outing together, Andrew O'Donnell took Randy on a trip to the downtown video arcade. When Randy returned, he seemed truly happy. Perhaps that was a promising sign. But what about the long term? What about the day Andrew O'Donnell completed his forty hours of community service and vanished from Randy's life?

This was the problem Kristin pondered later that evening as she and Randy finished washing and drying the supper dishes. Afterward the two of them proceeded to the living room. Kristin settled in an armchair with a mystery novel, while Randy sprawled on the floor to fiddle with his microscope. Holmes the cat eyed the cage of Watson the boa. Sherlock the dog, in turn, eyed Holmes. It was a portrait of domestic tranquillity that threatened at any moment to erupt in chaos.

Randy adjusted a slide in his microscope and squinted at it. 'Wow, this mold is really great,

Mom. Wanna take a look?'

Kristin knelt on the floor beside her son and peered into the microscope. She supposed the mold was lovely; the magnified spore sacks looked like puffy flowers on stems.

'Tomorrow we can start another experiment,' she said. 'We'll try growing some mold in the refrigerator this time and see what happens.'

'Yeah. And then we can show Andrew how to grow mold.'

Kristin smiled faintly. 'I'm not sure Andrew would be interested in mold.'

Randy's expression grew stolid, the way it did whenever Kristin implied that Andrew O'Donnell might be less than perfect.

'Andrew likes experiments,' Randy said. 'He wants me to show him how we make crystals in jars.' Randy went back to his microscope. Kristin picked up her book again, but she couldn't concentrate. She enjoyed sharing her love of science with Randy. It was a good pastime, one that drew them together—performing experiments, figuring out how things worked.

Kristin also liked the orderliness of science, the comforting knowledge that nature followed certain rules. Even a tornado or a hurricane could be explained by scientific principles. The trouble was people created emotional tornadoes and hurricanes without following any rules. A marriage that seemed unbreakable could suddenly shatter, a father could abandon his very own son—and a substitute dad could walk away when his forty hours were up, especially when he didn't want to be a substitute dad in the first place.

Kristin put down her book. 'Randy, you do realize that Mr. O'Donnell has a life of his own. He's a very busy man.'

'Sure, Mom,' Randy said with all the exaggerated patience of an eight-year-old. 'Andrew's always busy doing important things. But Saturday he's taking me to a baseball game.'

How could Randy be so attached to Andrew O'Donnell after only one outing? It scared Kristin. And Randy put out the red-alert signals every time Kristin tried to explain that Andrew wouldn't be around forever. She regretted ever signing up for this program!

Kristin riffled the pages of her mystery in frustration. She wouldn't mention anything more to Randy at the moment, but somehow she had to make him understand that Andrew O'Donnell's presence in their lives was only temporary. The sooner Randy accepted that, the less hurt he'd be when Andrew actually said goodbye.

Kristin glanced around her small living room, feeling cramped and restless in here. She knew she'd crowded too many objects into the room. A loyal person, she craved permanence, and it was difficult for her to throw anything

126

away. This meant she'd surrounded herself with remnants of the world she'd left behind: the flowerpots she'd hung in the windows of her Denver house, the whimsical ceramic cat that friends had given her when she graduated from veterinary school, the sewing machine on which she'd proven her utter inability to make clothes for an infant Randy. Kristin felt a sudden, sharp longing for the time in Colorado when she'd innocently believed her existence was complete. She'd had the perfect child, the perfect career, the perfect marriage. Or so she'd thought.

Kristin stood abruptly and surveyed the room, wishing she could throw out all the contents and start afresh. This move to Oklahoma was about starting afresh, after all. It was about giving herself and Randy a chance to begin again where they wouldn't be haunted by old memories.

Randy put another slide into his microscope and bent over it. 'This one's really gross,' he murmured to himself in obvious satisfaction. Kristin gave a genuine smile this time, reminding herself that she could still claim the perfect child and the perfect career. Two out of three wasn't so bad, was it? And surely she'd get used to this small town. Danfield offered distinct advantages: a safe atmosphere to raise her son, a community center with all manner of summer programs to keep Randy occupied while Kristin worked, a vet practice she had

127

taken over and could manage comfortably with the help of only one assistant. Kristin could look forward to a life in Danfield that was both fulfilling and relaxed in pace. What more did she want? Obstinately she ignored the ache of loneliness inside her. One thing she wouldn't look for in Danfield was another man, no matter how lonely she became.

A child's voice hollered from outside. 'Randy! Randy!'

Randy scrambled to his feet, microscope forgotten. 'That's Jonah,' he announced, charging from the house and making enough racket for ten boys. Kristin was glad that Randy had made a new friend, the nine-year-old next door. She went outside herself to enjoy the coolness of evening, Sherlock the sheepdog padding along beside her. Randy and Jonah pedaled down the street on their bicycles, and Jonah's mother, Pam, came to lean against the fence. Pam was a slight woman with wiry reddish hair. She and Kristin had already exchanged pleasantries several times, and it appeared she'd be a good neighbor.

'Hi,' Pam called. 'Settling in okay?'

'Getting there, Pam.' Kristin sauntered over to the fence and examined the peeling boards on her side. 'Know anybody who could give this a fresh coat of paint?'

'My husband's cousin is the local handyman. I'll tell him to pay you a visit.'

'I hope he does lawns, too,' Kristin

128

remarked. 'I'll put in the flower garden myself, though.' Kristin had always enjoyed gardening, drawn by every type of bloom: primrose, sweet William, iris, hollyhock. She liked knowing that plants she tended would flourish, then wither, then flourish again. It was a comforting pattern she could count on.

'I'll make sure I dig up some of my tulip bulbs for you,' Pam said now. 'So, how's Andrew O'Donnell working out as a substitute dad?'

Kristin restrained a grimace. Small towns possessed both advantages and disadvantages. Everybody seemed to know everybody else's business.

'Well, so far Andrew's been dependable with Randy,' Kristin said. 'Today he showed up when he said he would, and that's important.' She didn't voice her misgivings about Andrew; it was best to keep those private.

'I think this is the only way Andrew will ever be a father,' Pam said. 'That man never plans to settle down. I went to high school with him, you know. But he moved to Oklahoma City right after graduation. He always said he'd make a name for himself somewhere besides Danfield.'

'Hmm.' Kristin tried to remain noncommittal, but small-town gossip did hold a certain fascination, and Pam didn't need much encouragement to continue.

'Andrew's created quite a stir since coming

back last year,' Pam rattled on. 'O'Donnell's Fine Timepieces was almost going under before he took charge. If he can make the company profitable again, it'll be a real boost for Danfield. O'Donnell's used to be the biggest employer in town, you know. Of course, if anyone can save O'Donnell's, it'll be Andrew. I mean, look what he did with that bar in Oklahoma City. Bought it when the place was a shambles, and then turned it into the city's biggest night spot—O'Donnell's Country Western Dance Saloon. He'd bring in all the best bands from Nashville and really put on a show.'

Kristin lingered at the fence. 'If Andrew was such a success in Oklahoma City, it seems strange he'd come back to Danfield.'

'It seems strange to me, too,' Pam answered in a confidential tone. 'His family's watch factory was just about to go bankrupt—not real promising, you know? Andrew sold his saloon and put all his money into the factory. He could be looking at a bad loss if things don't work out.'

'No wonder he's so preoccupied all the time,' Kristin murmured, feeling an unexpected empathy for Andrew O'Donnell. 'I like the idea of his trying to rescue his family business. I hope it works out for him.'

'He could use a break. Believe me, since he got back to town, things have been hard for him with business—and with women, too,'

Pam added. 'He gets himself into more trouble! Before Judge Thaxter it was Connie, of Connie's Antiques. And before that it was Serena Morton. Serena was *not* serene when it came to Andrew, let me tell you. And before that—'

'Listen, Pam, I don't think I ought to know any more about Andrew's love life,' Kristin said hastily, her empathy for the man suddenly vanishing.

'It *is* an astonishing subject,' Pam conceded.

'Astonishing ... yes. Well, I'll look forward to those tulip bulbs. Thanks, Pam.' Kristin escaped back inside her house, sheepdog in tow. Enough of Andrew O'Donnell! She had other problems to worry about.

Kristin picked up Holmes, cradling the sleepy cat in her arms as she gazed out the window. Randy rode up and down the sidewalk on his bike with Jonah. Perhaps it was a coincidence, but Randy seemed a little more outgoing now that he'd gained a substitute father.

Kristin sighed and held the silky cat a little closer. 'Holmes, like it or not, from now on we do have to worry about Andrew O'Donnell. We have to worry about him a lot.'

*   *   *

The next week was a busy one for Kristin. She held her first vaccination clinic, attended a meeting of a regional wildlife foundation in nearby Oklahoma City and visited many of the farms outside Danfield to introduce herself as the new vet. Kristin found that if she kept herself occupied, her mind seemed to work better when trying to puzzle out a problem. And the problem of Andrew O'Donnell was, indeed, a puzzler. Randy seemed to be growing increasingly attached to the man. Kristin fervently wanted her son to be happy—but how dependent should she allow him to become on Andrew? So far she didn't have the answer.

Late one afternoon at the animal hospital, Kristin bent down, gathered a cocker spaniel in her arms and set him on the examining table. 'Don't give me that mournful look, Dessie,' she told the spaniel. 'You know this isn't going to hurt.' She raised one of Dessie's long ears, took a bottle and squeezed out four medicinal blue drops. Dessie continued to look sad; obviously he didn't like staying at the vet's to have his ear infection monitored.

'You and I, we both have our problems, Dessie,' Kristin muttered. 'But I'll wager mine are a whole lot worse than yours. Give me an ear infection any day over a court-ordered volunteer worming his way into my life.'

'Did I hear my name?' Andrew O'Donnell asked, poking his head through the doorway and giving Kristin a start. 'Better be careful. Your cat might get jealous if he hears you've been talking to a dog.'

Kristin patted Dessie's soft furry head. 'Mr. O'Donnell, if you must know, conversing with animals is an occupational hazard for a veterinarian.'

'Whatever you say.' Andrew smiled. Today he wore tan jeans and a vivid blue tie. As usual, his shirt pockets bristled with an assortment of pens and pencils. He looked good. Too good. Every time Kristin saw him he seemed more attractive, a disturbing phenomenon.

'Mr. O'Donnell, I expected you and Randy to return quite a while ago.'

Andrew came into the examining room, appearing only slightly apologetic. 'We got carried away at the arcade. They had a new game Randy liked. We both liked it, as a matter of fact. But Randy's out back in the kennels right now doing his chores.'

Kristin raised another spaniel ear and aimed her bottle. She rubbed both of Dessie's ears to work in the medicine, then quickly moved away.

'Stand back,' she warned Andrew.

'What—?'

The spaniel shook his head vigorously, long ears flapping like plane propellers and spraying the air with medicine drops. Then he settled down, ears floating back to resting position. It was safe to approach again.

Kristin awarded Dessie with a dog biscuit for his ordeal, and the spaniel wagged his stub of a tail when Andrew came over to pet him. It was annoying how children and dogs alike seemed to take to Andrew right off.

'We have to talk, Mr. O'Donnell.'

'Sure thing, Dr. Mabry.'

She gave him a hard glance. 'Mr. O'Donnell—'

'Why the formality? I think you could call me Andrew by now.' He leaned against the counter where Kristin had lined up her cotton swabs, vaccination tags and bottles of heartworm pills.

'Mr. O'Donnell, it's about Randy.'

'He's a good kid.'

Andrew O'Donnell was only making this task harder for her. 'Yes, Randy *is* a good kid. And that's why I don't want him hurt. You made it clear from the beginning that your schedule was very busy, and you were only volunteering under duress.'

'That doesn't mean I don't enjoy the time I spend with Randy. Sure, it stretches my schedule, but I'm trying to do a good job with him. Randy looks like you, by the way. Same nose, same blue eyes. I didn't realize before.' Andrew studied her as if seeking other similarities. Kristin straightened the collar of her lab coat, uncomfortable with his scrutiny. In this humid Oklahoma climate she still couldn't figure out what to do with her hair. Today she'd tried to keep it smoothed back from her face with a colorful scarf.

134

'Mr. O'Donnell,' she repeated firmly. 'Your way of doing a good job with Randy is the problem. First off, I understand you gave him a twenty-dollar bill the other day.'

Andrew shrugged. 'He saw a vintage comic he needed for his collection.'

'Things like that disrupt what I'm trying to teach Randy about money. He has an allowance that he earns with his chores.'

Andrew gave the cocker spaniel a good stomach rub. 'Okay, so I'll make the money a loan. How's that?'

'Just great. Now my son's in debt.' Kristin treated the spaniel to a good rub of her own. Dessie was so pleased with all the attention that he stuck his paws into the air. This conversation wasn't proceeding as Kristin would have liked, but she plowed ahead. 'Mr. O'Donnell, let's forget about the comic-book incident for a bit. We'll move on to the next incident.'

'Now I'm causing incidents?'

She gave him a disparaging look. 'Let's discuss last Saturday, when you took Randy to the movies. We're not talking single feature here. We're not even talking double feature. We're talking triple feature, Mr. O'Donnell! By the time Randy got home, he was in a daze from staring at a movie screen that long.'

'How often do you get a chance to see three classics in a row? You have to take these things as they come.'

'Right. Who'd want to miss *Curse of the Mummy, Son of the Mummy*, and *Return of the Mummy*?' Kristin watched as Andrew treated her to one of his grins. She realized she was getting nowhere fast with him. 'Mr. O'Donnell, marathon movie sessions are bad enough. But then you instigated the chili-dog episode ...'

'First it's an incident, now it's an episode,' he said. 'Let me guess. Next time you'll tell me I caused an entire event.'

She frowned at him. 'Randy got sick from eating too much when you took him to the carnival. He kept having nightmares about those chili dogs.'

Andrew finally had the decency to look regretful. 'So maybe I overindulged Randy a little that afternoon.'

'A little?' Kristin echoed. 'Unfortunately, I'm starting to figure out your philosophy. If a little is good, then a whole lot is better. But that doesn't work with an eight-year-old, Mr. O'Donnell. Randy needs a father right now, not a friend. Someone who'll set boundaries he can count on. That's what being a parent is all about, even if you're only a substitute parent. And even if you'll simply disappear from his life when your forty hours are up!'

Silence followed Kristin's outburst. The spaniel put his head on his paws and looked mournful again. Andrew straightened from the counter, and after a long moment he spoke.

'Dr. Mabry—Kristin. I've noticed something odd. Randy never talks about his real dad. Not a mention. Not a word.'

Kristin turned away and busied herself recapping Dessie's medicine bottle. 'What happened with my ex-husband isn't something you need to concern yourself with.'

Andrew didn't say anything, but simply waited. Kristin could feel him waiting, even though she refused to look at him. She twisted the bottle in her hands, turning the cap too tight.

'Very well,' she said at last in a low voice. 'Randy's father remarried shortly after ... after the divorce. In a matter of weeks, really. He's already started a new family, and he doesn't want any complications from his first marriage—not even from his son. Of course Randy's taken it hard. He doesn't understand.'

'I don't understand, either.' Andrew sounded harsh. 'What kind of man would abandon his own kid?'

Kristin set the medicine bottle very carefully on the counter. She told herself that if she kept all her motions careful and precise, she'd get through this conversation just fine.

'I've asked myself the exact same question over and over. I've asked myself a lot of questions like that. But for Randy's sake, I won't ever say anything bad about his father in front of him. He's confused enough as it is.'

Andrew gazed across the examination table

at Kristin. 'This volunteer program is supposed to be temporary, any way you look at it. Only a stopgap until a kid can have a real father.'

'I'm never getting married again,' she said. 'Another marriage isn't the solution! Randy could be hurt even worse than before. What's to stop another husband from walking out? Anyway, I just can't risk it.'

Andrew went on studying her intently. 'Sounds to me like Randy wasn't the only one hurt. But you can't possibly expect this volunteer program to be a permanent solution.'

'I *did* expect it to be a solution. It seemed perfectly feasible—until you showed up, that is.' Suddenly Kristin felt downright miserable. She was trying so hard to protect her son, but the harder she tried, the more she exposed him to potential pain. She gathered the cocker spaniel in her arms and lifted him from the table. 'We're finished here,' she said to Dessie. 'And it looks like you and I are finished talking, too, Mr. O'Donnell. For now, all I'm asking is that you set a few rules with Randy. Set some limits.'

'You're going to trust me to do a good job?' he asked, his tone just a bit caustic.

'I still have strong misgivings about you. With Randy, it's different. He seems to have taken a liking to you from the first moment he saw you. Anyway, goodbye, Mr. O'Donnell. I suppose Randy will see you tomorrow.'

'I'll be here, right on schedule.'

That was one thing about Andrew. He always showed up right on schedule. He'd never once let Randy down.

'We'll see you tomorrow, then, Mr. O'Donnell.'

'Call me Andrew,' he said.

'Goodbye ... Mr. O'Donnell!'

CHAPTER THREE

As Kristin hurried along Main Street in downtown Danfield, it seemed as if every surface was made of brick: brick sidewalks, brick streets and brick office buildings, all tinged a mellow cinnamon color in the late-afternoon sunlight. Kristin was reminded of a sepia photograph. In fact, she half imagined she'd stepped into an old photograph herself, traveling back to the turn of the century.

Kristin stopped in front of the O'Donnell building. It was an impressive structure, three stories high, ornate molding all the way around the roof. Dark green awnings shaded the windows, and stone pots overflowing with violets and dahlias created a bright welcome on either side of the door. O'Donnell's Fine Timepieces was scripted in gilt lettering on the window, contributing to the overall impression of nostalgic elegance. It was all very admirable. Kristin wished she could admire the building's proprietor, too, but this time the man had gone too far.

She pushed open the door and found herself in a showroom of polished wood cases and walls covered in creamy, faintly embossed paper. Her gaze was immediately drawn to Andrew O'Donnell. Seated in his office, a glassed-off portion of the showroom, he was deep in conversation on the phone, at the same time sorting through the jumble of papers on his desk. He looked quite preoccupied, but then he glanced up and saw Kristin. After a few moments he got off the phone and came out of his office. Every time Kristin saw him, she found new details about his appearance that attracted her. This afternoon, for instance, she noted that although his hair was a shade of rich, smoky black, it also held just a hint of dark russet.

'Doc Mabry. Come for a tour of the facilities?' he said teasingly. 'I took Randy all through the place this morning—showed him how a watch was made, start to finish. He's smart. Catches on real quick, whatever I tell him.'

'Yes, he does,' Kristin said. 'That seems to be the problem.'

Andrew looked amused. 'Figured you didn't come here to pass the time of day. I wonder what I've done now.'

'You can't guess?' she asked.

'I've been a model substitute father these past few days,' he said with an air of piety. 'No cash advances, no chili dogs. I can't think what more you want from me.' Andrew ushered her into his office. It had an open, inviting atmosphere. The blinds were drawn up at the window to let the sun in, and the walls were lined with prints of Danfield's frontier days: scenes of horses and buggies stirring up dust on Main Street, a few portraits of grim-faced settlers standing proudly in front of their log cabins.

Andrew motioned Kristin into a chair and then settled behind his desk. 'Fire away,' he said. 'What's my latest transgression?'

'Look, Andrew, I really don't enjoy bringing up all these problems. That's one of the reasons I'm a vet. I like being around animals, instead of trying to manage people all day.'

'I knew you'd do it sooner or later,' he said.

He'd made her lose her train of thought. 'What are you talking about?'

'I knew eventually you'd call me Andrew. That being my name and all.'

She made another attempt to get through to the man. 'Mr. O'Donnell—Andrew, I'm just trying to say I didn't really want to come down here and have this discussion with you. It's not something I've been looking forward to.'

'So let's not have it,' he suggested amenably. 'We'll talk about watches instead.' He rummaged through his desk and brought out an oversize pocket watch. Clicking it open, he revealed the intricate inner workings. 'This is a demo, so it should be easy to see. Randy enjoyed tinkering with it this morning. That's the ratchet wheel, right there. Meshes perfectly with the crown wheel, if I do say so myself. And here's the rocker spring—'

'Very impressive. But it still doesn't change the fact that you taught my eight-year-old son how to play poker, and then you let him drive your car. Next thing I know, he'll come home smoking cigars and betting on horses!'

Andrew clicked his watch shut and slid back in his chair. 'You can relax. I don't like cigars and I never cared much for this idea of racing a bunch of horses around a track.'

'Mr. O'Donnell, would you stop being so damn difficult!'

'Andrew, remember?'

'Dammit, Andrew—'

'No, just Andrew.' A look of satisfaction came over his features now. 'Although my father used to say, "Dammit, Andrew," an awful lot when I was growing up.'

Kristin groaned and tried again. 'Andrew, listen. Today my eight-year-old son came home bragging that he'd won a poker hand with a straight flush. He also said he'd been tooling around town at the wheel of your Bronco. Can't you understand why I might be just a little bit disturbed by all this?'

'You really are blowing things out of proportion,' Andrew said, his tone reasonable. 'Here's what happened. Randy asked me what I do in my spare time, and I told him about my weekly poker game. So of course he asked me how to play, and naturally I ended up giving him a few pointers.'

'Naturally.'

Kristin's sarcasm seemed lost on Andrew. 'As for the driving episode, it was perfectly safe,' he went on. 'I took Randy to a dirt road where there wasn't any traffic, and I taught him how to steer and how to shift gears. I even showed him the basics of defensive driving— never tailgate, expect the unexpected, take responsibility for anything that might happen. Randy's old enough to start learning these things.'

Kristin drummed her fingers impatiently on the arms of her chair. 'You're missing the whole point. Maybe you think two-year-olds should have their own sports cars, I don't know. If that's your opinion, I suppose you're entitled to it. But Randy's my son, and where he's concerned you have to abide by *my* opinions. Get it?'

'I'm starting to get it, all right,' he said slowly. 'You want to have this both ways. You want a substitute father around, but you don't want him to be a real person, with ideas and thoughts of his own. Maybe I'm crazy, but I see a few kinks in your plan.'

Kristin stood and crossed to the window to gaze out at the dazzling blue Oklahoma sky. She'd come here today more than ready to confront Andrew, eager to tell him exactly what he was doing wrong with her son. But confronting Andrew hadn't seemed to help in the least. She only felt more restless and uneasy.

'I know Randy needs a different perspective than mine, a male perspective,' she admitted. 'But since my divorce I'm through trying to deal with men. That's why I got Randy involved in this program—so I wouldn't *have* to deal with men.'

Andrew walked over to stand beside her, leaning against the window frame. He regarded her for a long moment. 'That guy you married, Kristin. He really left you with some serious scars, didn't he?'

'We're talking about Randy, not me,' she protested.

'It sure seems like we're talking about you.'

She stuffed her hands into the pockets of her skirt, curling her fingers tightly. 'What happened in my marriage doesn't have anything to do with your role as substitute father.'

'What do you plan, Kristin—to keep all the parts of your life in separate boxes? It can't work that way. Your attitude about men is bound to affect Randy sooner or later.'

'I don't have any particular attitude about

men. I mean, that's really an annoying phrase—"Attitude about men."'

'Looks like I've touched a nerve,' he said. 'Let me see if I have this right. You've decided all men are jerks like your ex-husband, so you've tried to come up with a father figure for your son who can't threaten either you or Randy in any way. Problem is, I'm the father figure, and from the very beginning I haven't toed the line. Am I leaving anything out?'

'You've just about covered it,' she said, trying to mock him. But Andrew was, indeed, prodding too close to painful emotions. Once she'd believed that a man and a woman could fall in love and stay in love forever. She'd been an optimist by nature, an idealist. However, she'd recently become a cynic about the possibility of 'forever' with any man.

'I suppose you think I should've run right out after my divorce and jumped into another man's arms,' she said scornfully.

'Why not?'

'I'll tell you why not. Men don't exactly flock around a divorcee who has a child to support.'

'I don't buy that,' Andrew murmured. 'You're a beautiful woman, Kristin. Plenty of men have probably flocked around.'

His gaze held hers. Kristin had managed to remain aloof from men in the months since her divorce, but no man had looked at her as Andrew was now. His dark gray eyes seemed to guard a tenderness, a dangerous warmth. All she could do was go on standing there, too aware of him next to her, both bathed in the sunshine spilling through the window. His tie was casually loosened, his shirt a cool blue cotton that had an inviting look about it. In fact, everything about Andrew seemed inviting at that moment ...

He reached out to smooth an unruly strand of hair from her cheek, his fingers brushing her skin. His touch was gentle. 'Kristin,' he said at last in a musing tone. 'Kristin, you *are* beautiful.'

'Don't, Andrew. Don't say things like that to me—please.'

He smiled. 'You have too many rules. Rules for Randy, rules for me, probably all sorts of rules for yourself.'

'I need rules.' She couldn't think straight, gazing into Andrew's eyes like this. She had trembled to his touch, and she was still trembling inside as Andrew leaned toward her ...

Someone tapped against one of the glass panes surrounding Andrew's office. Too late Kristin realized how exposed the two of them were. She stepped back quickly and saw a trim man of sixty or so waiting outside the office, a bland expression on his face. Too bland an expression—it was likely the gentleman had seen everything.

Andrew's demeanor became businesslike, and he tightened the knot of his tie. 'That's Mr.

Larcum out there, my five-o'clock appointment. A very important appointment, by the way, but you almost made me forget about it.'

'Don't worry. I was just leaving.' Kristin escaped out the door, taking with her a disturbing knowledge. If not for the interruption, Andrew might have kissed her today. But even more disturbing was the realization that she'd wanted him to kiss her. She'd wanted it very much.

* * *

'No way, Andrew. No how. I can't believe you're even asking me something like this. You actually want me to go on a date with you? Are you crazy?' Kristin gripped the telephone receiver, pacing back and forth over the rag rug in her living room. Her visit to Andrew O'Donnell's office the other day had been unsettling enough. Now she was so agitated by his phone call that she couldn't sit still. She was grateful that Randy was outside playing. She certainly didn't need her son to overhear her conversation with Andrew.

'Stop leaping to conclusions,' Andrew said grouchily from the other end of the line. 'I'm not asking you out on a date. It's more like a business meeting.'

'You just said it was a cocktail party.'

'Okay, okay, it's a cocktail party for some of

my business associates.'

Kristin continued to pace. 'Andrew, I'm not your business associate.'

'Hear me out, will you?' he asked. 'I'm in a real bind. The party's at my place. I have to give the blasted thing so I can introduce some important people around.'

Kristin glared at the telephone receiver. 'You know, I wondered why Randy's been saying "blasted" this and "blasted" that all the time. I should've figured it was your influence. Goodbye, Andrew—'

'Don't hang up. I need you to go to this party with me. Not as a date. More like ... an acquaintance. That's it. I need you to go as my acquaintance.'

Kristin struggled to remain calm. In the few days since her visit to O'Donnell's Fine Timepieces, she'd seen Andrew once, briefly. He'd come to the house to pick up Randy for another outing to the movies—this time a single feature, although Andrew had taken Randy for an ice-cream sundae afterward. Kristin had tabulated the hours left in Andrew's community-service obligation and realized he was rapidly fulfilling his quota. She'd therefore sat down with her son and reminded him frankly that Andrew O'Donnell was only a temporary substitute. Her words had made little impact. Randy stubbornly continued to believe that Andrew would be a permanent fixture in the Mabry household.

148

Now, to top things off, Andrew had called and was making this completely unsuitable request.

'Andrew,' Kristin said, 'I understand you have a reputation for alienating half the female population of Danfield. Not only are we talking about Judge Loraine Thaxter, but there's Connie, of Connie's Antiques, and one Serena Morton who is *not* so serene when it comes to you—'

'Is there a point to this?' he asked.

'Yes, there is. I realize that your romantic career in Danfield has been ... bumpy. But surely you can find at least one unsuspecting woman out there who hasn't heard about your reputation and who'd be willing to go to your cocktail party.'

'About this reputation of mine,' Andrew said. 'It's overrated. So I've had a few misunderstandings with the opposite sex. Could happen to anyone.'

'Misunderstandings ... hmm. Sounds like the understatement of the century.' Carrying the phone, Kristin plopped down on the couch and swung her feet onto the coffee table. She watched as the parakeet, Hercule Poirot, fluffed his feathers importantly in his cage.

'I'll tell you the problem,' Andrew said, growing eloquent. 'The problem is that you start out taking a woman to a play or an art exhibit, and next thing you know she's choosing a china pattern and ordering wedding invitations. Then, when you fail to see the connection between a simple, ordinary date and happily-ever-after, the woman impounds your gun collection or threatens to toss you out of her antique store.'

Obviously this subject was one of some concern to Andrew. Kristin settled back a little more on her overstuffed couch. Sherlock chose this moment to lumber onto the couch beside her. Luckily it was a big, sturdy piece of furniture with room for all. Not to be outdone, Holmes leapt up to defend Kristin's other side. Dog and cat regarded each other warily across Kristin's lap. She patted each animal in turn and then gazed across the room at the cedar hope chest she'd inherited from her grandmother, the burnished wood complemented by a vintage needlepoint cushion. Women and their everlasting hope chests...

'Andrew, let me clue you in on something,' Kristin said. 'Unfortunately, the female of our species is raised to believe in happily-ever-after with a man. You just have to consider that fact when you start taking a woman to plays and art galleries. It can't be all that much of a surprise to you. I mean, you seem to think *I* should get married again—as if it's my destiny somehow.'

'Some people need to be married,' he said in a guarded tone. 'I just don't happen to be one of them.'

150

She sat up straight. 'I don't happen to be one of them, either. Which brings us back to the fact that I'm not going to your damn cocktail party!'

'Ever wonder if maybe Randy gets his bad language from you?' Andrew asked.

'Good*bye*, Andrew.' Kristin plunked the receiver down, but went on staring at the phone. Just as she'd known it would, it rang a few moments later. She grabbed up the receiver.

'I already said no, Andrew. N-o. How can I be any more straightforward than that?'

'I'm asking this as a favor,' he persisted. 'The party starts at eight tomorrow night. I don't have a lot of time to negotiate.'

'If you're the one who planned the party, why didn't you think ahead about arranging a date for it?'

'Like I told you, this isn't a date,' he muttered. 'It's a business gathering. And under these particular circumstances, you're the one I need at the party. You're the only woman who'll do.'

'Why? Because I'm the only woman in Danfield who is still speaking to you?' Kristin was exasperated. 'You're making this sound mysterious. I wish I knew what you were up to, Andrew.'

'It's a long story. Why can't you just say yes and be done with it? Besides, you and I need to spend more time together to talk about

151

Randy.'

Andrew knew right where to hit her. All he had to do was mention her son and she began to waver. She swung her feet down from the coffee table, maneuvering away from her furry companions on the sofa. She took the phone over to the window. Lifting the lace curtain, she could see Randy running across the lawn, playing a rough-and-tumble version of tag with Jonah and two other neighborhood kids. Randy seemed so much happier lately, as if the combination of Oklahoma and Andrew O'Donnell was making him flourish.

'You still there, Kristin?' Andrew said.

She sighed. 'Yes . . . yes, I'm still here. This is against my better judgement and I don't know why I'm doing it, but you can pick me up at seven-thirty tomorrow night. I'll go to your party. Just remember, though—this *isn't* a date!'

CHAPTER FOUR

The next evening at twenty after seven, Kristin rushed to get ready for her non-date with Andrew O'Donnell. She couldn't find the belt to her dress, she hadn't brushed her hair yet, and she didn't even know what shoes she was going to wear. It had been a wild day. She'd held another vaccination clinic and then ended up performing emergency surgery on a collie hit by a car. The collie, fortunately, had pulled through, and was resting at the hospital under the supervision of Kristin's capable assistant, a fifty-year-old woman who'd worked for the previous vet. Kristin herself had barely reached home in time to make supper. Now she rooted frantically through her untidy closet in search of shoes. Randy hovered nearby.

'Maybe Andrew will take you to the movies,' he said.

'Randy, I told you this isn't a date,' she answered as patiently as possible. 'Andrew and I are going to a business function.' She unearthed an aged magenta pump and a white sandal, tossing both aside. Sometimes her inability to throw anything away really got on her nerves. Goodness, here were the basketball shoes she'd worn in high school!

'You never go on dates, Mom.'

This observation distracted her from footgear. She poked her head out of the closet and gazed at her son.

'Look, Randy, I have a certain philosophy about dating ...' Kristin hesitated. Perhaps it was better not to get into philosophical theory with her eight-year-old. 'I'm not going to start dating Andrew, that's one thing for sure.'

'I like Andrew,' Randy said, a stubborn look on his face. Kristin wished she had time to argue with him. But she'd already bluntly stated several times that Andrew O'Donnell wouldn't be around forever. Her son refused to listen, no matter what she said.

It didn't help that at the moment Kristin was dithering about the right shoes to wear, behaving exactly as if she *were* going on a date with Andrew. That would only encourage Randy's hopes. Already Kristin heartily regretted agreeing to this party of Andrew's!

The doorbell rang, and Randy hurtled out of the room to answer it. Still berating herself, Kristin grabbed a pair of black pumps and slipped them on her feet. She found her belt in a corner of the closet, yanked a brush through her hair and then thoroughly dismayed herself by dabbing perfume behind her ears. Before she could do anything else reckless, she hurried out to the living room.

Randy and Andrew O'Donnell stood beside the terrarium, engrossed in conversation. Randy was giving an elaborate description of his pet boa Watson, and Andrew listened gravely, interjecting appropriate comments from time to time. Kristin watched the two of them. They seemed so comfortable together: one small, sturdy boy with corn-blond hair flopped over his forehead, one tall, sturdy man with dark hair waving *back* from his forehead. Watching them, Kristin felt an odd tightness in her throat. It was a moment or two before she stepped farther into the room.

'Randy, Jonah's waiting for you next door,' she said. 'Jonah's mom says she'll make popcorn for the two of you tonight.' Even the promise of popcorn couldn't tear Randy away from Andrew's side. Kristin had to prod Randy firmly out the door, waiting to make certain he went into Pam's house. Then she turned back to Andrew.

He looked particularly handsome tonight. Instead of his usual jeans, he wore a light sports jacket and casual trousers. His diamond-patterned tie in burgundy and ivory added exactly the right touch of elegance.

Kristin had a need to keep moving. She was afraid that if she slowed down, she wouldn't know what to say to Andrew. She waved him toward the couch.

'I'll just be a minute. Make yourself comfortable.' She hoped he'd be able to find a place to sit among Randy's games and books and model cars. She and Randy ought to have cleaned the house a little, but too late now. Besides, Andrew had seen the clutter here before. Why was she behaving as if tonight was something different—a special occasion?

Followed by dog and cat, Kristin searched for her purse and finally located it underneath a chair in the dining room. Next she fastened her electronic pager to her belt in case any pet owners needed to reach her. But nothing else remained to be done. At last she had no choice. She had to return to the living room to face Andrew.

He'd found an empty spot on the couch,

after all, and was studying the jigsaw puzzle Randy and Kristin had started to assemble on the coffee table. He put a piece into place and then gazed at Kristin.

'You look nice,' he said.

'You don't have to be polite or anything. Just because we're going to this party—'

'I'm not being polite. I'm telling you the truth. You look nice.'

'Well ... thank you.' Suddenly she was glad she'd chosen one of her more flattering dresses, a red silk print that draped her body in soft curves and folds. And she'd discovered recently that the less she did with her hair in this new climate, the better. Tonight it had hardly seen a brush, yet it fell with a natural curl to her shoulders. Kristin only wished that she didn't care so much what Andrew thought of her.

He still hadn't moved from the couch. He looked rather brooding as he examined another piece of the jigsaw puzzle.

'Shall we go?' she said. 'You don't want to be late to your own party. The funny thing is, it doesn't seem like you really want to go to it.'

He stirred, picking up one of Randy's model cars and turning it around in his hand. 'Usually I don't mind social gatherings.'

'What's different about tonight? You know, Andrew, ever since you mentioned this party you've been acting strangely. I don't like it.'

Andrew stood and headed for the door. 'It's

just a damn party,' he said with an air of determination. 'Come on, let's go.'

He was acting more peculiar by the minute. Kristin allowed him to usher her outside, but she truly regretted this venture. What kind of evening could possibly await her?

*   *   *   *here*

'Sherlock the sheepdog, Holmes the cat, Watson the snake—where's Professor Moriarty?' Andrew asked.

It was only a short drive to his house, yet the man seemed determined to pry into Kristin's life as much as possible along the way. 'If you must know, Moriarty's passed on,' Kristin said. 'The professor was a goldfish, and one day Holmes took matters into his own hands—or his own paws.'

'Your cat ate your fish?' Andrew was laughing now. 'Holmes finally got Moriarty, eh? A fitting end to that master criminal.'

Andrew seemed awfully pleased with his humor. By now they'd arrived at his home, an old brick house that suggested far-off lands. The flared slope of the eaves evoked a Japanese pagoda, while the red-tiled roof put Kristin in mind of a Spanish villa—yet the wide front porch bespoke the American prairie. The combination was charming.

'My grandparents built this place in the 1930s,' Andrew said as he walked Kristin up to the door. 'When I moved back to Danfield, I decided I couldn't let the house go out of the family, so I settled here myself.'

'You really have a history in Danfield,' Kristin said.

'When I was growing up, I took it for granted—all my family heritage. But now ... now it's different.' Andrew frowned, as if reluctant to reveal too much of himself. Or maybe it was the thought of his party that made him look so displeased.

As he ushered Kristin into the house, she saw that the get-together was already under way, people milling around, sampling the delicacies laid out by caterers. The proceedings were being supervised by Andrew's secretary, Ginnie, a stylish older woman with cropped gray hair who gave Kristin a rather sympathetic nod when introduced.

'Dr. Mabry, so you're the brave soul,' Ginnie said. 'Congratulations, my dear, and good luck.'

Andrew took Kristin's elbow and steered her in a new direction.

'What was that about?' Kristin demanded. 'Why did your secretary say those things?'

'Don't mind Ginnie,' he said with forced heartiness. 'She gets carried away, that's all. Here's someone else I want you to meet.'

Andrew began introducing Kristin right and left, giving her no time to ponder his secretary's peculiar remarks. Kristin learned that most of the guests were employees of O'Donnell's Fine Timepieces. She might even have started to enjoy herself, but Andrew never let her stay put for more than a minute. He'd introduce her to someone, barely give her time to begin a chat and then he'd haul her off again.

Finally Kristin marched over to the buffet table and served herself a chocolate éclair. Andrew stayed close, seeming almost protective of her.

'You're acting stranger all the time,' she complained. 'What on earth is going on, Andrew? Why won't you let me talk to anyone?'

'You've talked to plenty of people,' he said. 'I'm just trying to make sure you ... circulate.'

'I've been circulating so much my head's spinning.'

'Maybe this wasn't such a good idea,' he muttered. 'Bringing you here at all.'

An odd thing for him to say, considering he'd practically twisted her arm to get her here. 'You know, Andrew, I do possess a little bit of social etiquette, if you'd just let me use it. You don't need to be ashamed of me.'

'Who said anything about being ashamed?' he asked. 'You're the best damn looking woman in this room. Under other circumstances I'd be showing you off.'

This compliment from him was perplexing, to say the least. 'Whatever is wrong with you?' she demanded. 'You're having a party at your own house and you act like the place is booby-trapped!'

'That's a good word for it. Come on. I think we both need a time-out.'

Kristin didn't need a time-out. She'd barely had a chance to get her bearings, but Andrew seemed to be following his own peculiar agenda tonight. He pulled Kristin away from the festivities and led her toward the back of the house. Regretfully, she left her chocolate éclair behind. A moment later she found herself in a large room with French doors opening to a garden. She felt immediately drawn toward the garden: lovely beds of roses, bellflowers and pink turtle-heads. Gazing in delight, she was almost willing to forgive Andrew his irritating behavior.

'Did you plant all this yourself?' she asked, standing at the French doors to savor the twilight and the fragrant breeze.

'Not a twig of it. Tulips, turnips—they're all the same to me. That's the handiwork of a man who used to work for my grandparents and still insists on keeping the grounds for me. He's pretty spry for eighty-five. I think digging around in soil keeps him young.'

'It's a wonderful pastime.' Kristin felt oddly disappointed that it wasn't Andrew's pastime. She loved gardening, and for a brief moment she'd enjoyed the thought of sharing an enthusiasm with him.

She turned back into the room and saw that

it was half den, half workshop. In addition to a sturdy couch, a few armchairs and an elaborate stereo system, a long workbench took pride of place against one of the walls. It was flanked by no-nonsense tool cabinets and presided over by a heavy-duty fluorescent lamp.

Andrew had followed the direction of Kristin's gaze. 'That's where I do my tinkering,' he explained. 'Whenever I get a chance, I poke around at flea markets and antique stores, anyplace I might find an old broken-down watch that needs my services. Nothing's better than rehabilitating some forgotten timepiece.'

He made a watch sound as if it were a living thing, the tick of its innards rather like a heartbeat. Kristin couldn't help smiling at that. She crossed to the workbench and saw an impressive array of equipment: a lathe, a bench vise, sets of files and gauges.

'I'd say you do a bit more than tinker,' she remarked. 'This is all very professional.'

'I grew up helping my grandfather and then my father. I learned from them how it should be done.'

Kristin sat down on the stool in front of the workbench and wondered what it would have been like to grow up surrounded with a family heritage like this. Her own family was scattered: her parents in Illinois, a grandfather in Montana. None of her relatives had ever stayed long enough in one place to establish roots, as the O'Donnells had done. She envied Andrew.

'I can see why you came back to Danfield,' she told him. 'You have something to anchor you here.'

He gave a sardonic smile. 'I sure didn't think so when I was younger. I couldn't wait to get out of this little town. And forget the family business—I left that to my father and my uncle. It was damn exciting, taking a risk in Oklahoma City and seeing if I could make a go of that saloon—something completely different than watchmaking.' Andrew's expression grew reflective. 'But then, not too long ago, everything changed. My father died, and my uncle just couldn't keep the factory going on his own. He asked me if I wanted to take over—and there was the choice. Sell the company, or try to make it something special again, the way it was when my great-grandfather started it. Even though the stakes were high, I couldn't resist the challenge.'

'Something special,' Kristin echoed, liking the sound of those words. 'Is it turning out the way you wanted, Andrew?'

He prowled the room. 'Hell, it hasn't been easy so far. My father and my uncle made the mistake of trying to make inexpensive digital watches. But other manufacturers can produce those far more cheaply and in far greater volume than we can.' Andrew grew more intense, stopping in front of Kristin to tap the

162

workbench for emphasis. 'I'll tell you what I've been doing. I've returned to the original O'Donnell timepiece—the old-fashioned mechanical watch. Expensive, to be sure, but well crafted. There should be a selectivity, a perception of exclusiveness about owning an O'Donnell timepiece. That's the niche I want to carve out for my great-grandfather's company.'

Kristin could sense Andrew's vision. 'You're talking about something that could really catch on. People want old-fashioned quality.'

'I've had to revamp the entire company— buy different machinery, retrain employees, change the layout of the factory. It's taken a big investment, and I need to make damn sure it pays off.'

'You've convinced me already,' she said. 'I'd certainly wear one of your timepieces.'

He studied her. 'A pendant watch would suit you,' he murmured. 'Chiseled gold, because your hair's gold ...'

His words sounded intimate. Perhaps too intimate. Kristin stood quickly and went to peruse the empty gun cabinets mounted to the walls.

'I suppose Judge Thaxter won't let you have your firearms back,' she said, wondering why this reminder of Andrew's volatile love life nettled her so. Why couldn't she just be amused by his romantic escapades and dismiss them?

'The judge thinks I need to learn a lesson,'

Andrew said gruffly. 'Something about family responsibility. At least, that's what she said. If you ask me, she was just steamed because I wouldn't sign the marriage license.'

'Are you still seeing her?' Kristin asked, dismayed at herself for letting this question pop out of her mouth.

Now Andrew looked truly sour. 'No, I'm not seeing her. I'm not seeing anybody. I learn from my mistakes. No more women.'

'I learn from my mistakes, too,' Kristin said. 'No more men. I guess we have something in common, after all, Andrew.'

'That's where you're wrong. Randy needs a father, and you need a husband. It's plain as anything.'

Kristin stared at him in annoyance. What made Andrew O'Donnell think he could make such ready assumptions about her? 'One husband was more than enough,' she said. 'And I should've known better than to fall in love in the first place. I was too young, too naive ... You know, Andrew, you can stop me anytime. You don't actually have to listen to my life story.'

He settled down at the workbench, loosening his tie. 'I don't have anything better to do right now.'

'No, you just have a whole houseful of guests.'

'Ginnie is handling everything in her usual efficient way,' he said. 'And maybe you need to talk about some of this. Get it out in the open for once.'

'I'm not going to give you a dissertation on my private life,' Kristin protested. 'Besides, you're just looking for an excuse to avoid your own party.'

'I think I just figured something out,' he said in a musing tone. 'Randy never talks about what's really bothering him—the fact that his father doesn't want him anymore. Maybe Randy learned that trait from you. Kristin, do you ever talk about what's really on your mind?'

The only thing on Kristin's mind at the moment was a sincere desire to escape back home to her son, her cat, her dog and other assorted creatures who didn't ask difficult questions.

'Randy knows he can talk to me about anything that's bothering him,' she said defensively. 'You really do make too many assumptions.'

'Maybe I'm just a little curious about what's going on in your head. But you're so damn prickly. You've got the barricades up so high nobody can see over them. What did that guy do to you, anyway, the guy you married?'

Kristin turned and stared out toward the garden again. The summer dusk was heavy and sweet, enveloping her. And all of a sudden it seemed very difficult to keep her feelings inside.

CHAPTER FIVE

'My husband was unfaithful to me,' Kristin said, her voice low. 'It turned out he'd been having an affair for quite some time. And then he left me for this other woman.'

Out in the garden, a hummingbird hovered with a bright flash of wings, only to dart away again. Andrew didn't say anything for a moment, then he came over to Kristin and touched her shoulder.

'I'm sorry,' he said quietly. 'I didn't realize it was like that.'

She didn't want his sympathy, and she stepped away from him. When she spoke, she managed a brittle amusement. 'It's ironic, really, the way it happened. You see, my husband and I ran a vet clinic together, and the woman he had an affair with was our twenty-year-old assistant. I mean, it *is* funny, when you think about it.'

Kristin was prodding a wound that hadn't yet healed, and meanwhile Andrew was still gazing at her with his damned sympathy. But she couldn't seem to stop talking. Now that she'd begun, it was almost a relief to tell the rest of it.

'I started out as an assistant to Blake myself,' she continued. 'That's how I met him. I married him, went through veterinary school so we could run the clinic together—it seemed the ideal partnership. Of course, I didn't realize that Blake had a tendency to romance his assistants. I didn't realize I was part of a pattern, for goodness' sake!'

Kristin paused, but she couldn't really stop now. It all had to come out. 'I should have seen the signs,' she said brusquely. 'They were certainly there. The way Blake stopped showing affection to me. The way he grew distant to Randy. I was just so determined to keep my perfect world intact I wouldn't face how imperfect it actually was. The truth is, I'm much better off now. Randy is the one good thing that came out of my marriage. I have my son, and I have a brand-new life. You don't need to feel sorry for me, Andrew.'

He stepped close to her again. 'Kristin ...' Andrew didn't say anything more. In the most natural way imaginable, he pulled Kristin gently into his arms. He offered a silent comfort she couldn't resist. She leaned against him, savoring his strength, taking in the clean smell of his cologne, a scent that reminded her of cool, dark woodlands. But then Andrew tilted her chin and kissed her, offering sweet danger now, not comfort. She allowed herself only one brief taste of his lips before she struggled away.

'Dammit, Andrew!' Her voice shook. 'I don't need this.'

He frowned. 'I don't need this, either. I don't

know what the hell I'm doing with you, or why.'

Kristin struggled to compose herself. She needed to escape the intimate atmosphere of this room. 'There *is* a party going on out there, no matter how much you try to ignore it,' she said.

He continued gazing at her with a slight frown, making it obvious he wasn't satisfied to leave matters as they were. But he didn't press her any further.

'Sure,' he said at last. 'I guess we'd better get out there.' He straightened his tie like someone tightening a noose. Then he ushered her from the room and toward the front of the house. More guests had arrived, and Andrew went right back to his bewildering tactics. He'd introduce Kristin to someone, barely give her a chance to say hello, and then he'd drag her off in a new direction, moving along at a confusing pace. To make matters worse, Kristin was still unsettled by his kiss.

'Slow down,' she told him. 'All these faces are a blur and I can't remember anybody's name.'

'Have to keep moving. Believe me, we can't afford to stand still.'

Kristin was more puzzled than ever by his attitude, but he gave her no opportunity to ask questions. They reached another guest who'd just arrived, and Kristin recognized this one as the gentleman she'd glimpsed outside

Andrew's office a few days before. Andrew launched into greetings and introductions without wasting any time.

'Kristin, I'd like you to meet Mr. Benjamin Larcum. Mr. Larcum, this is Kristin Mabry.'

Mr. Larcum was a spruce-looking man, giving the impression he allowed himself no excesses. Dressed in a neat suit, he was unmarred by the slightest rumple, a crisp white handkerchief folded into his breast pocket. His gray hair was springy, yet he had combed it firmly from a precise part. His gaze was keen, as if he might be on the lookout for anything that needed tidying up.

'So you're Dr. Mabry,' he said. 'It's a pleasure to meet you. Andrew has told me so much about you.'

'He has?' Disconcerted, she glanced at Andrew.

'Mr. Larcum knows all about your being the new vet in town,' Andrew said, his voice just a shade too hearty. He took hold of her elbow. 'If you'll excuse us, Mr. Larcum, I need to introduce Kristin to a few other people.'

'We're not in that much of a rush,' she said. This time she wouldn't let Andrew drag her off before she'd almost had a chance to say two words. She ignored the way he was nudging her, and she smiled at Mr. Larcum.

'Tell me, are you associated with O'Donnell's Fine Timepieces?' she asked.

Mr. Larcum took on a judicial air. 'Not at

the moment, Dr. Mabry. But very soon I'll be deciding if Larcum Department Stores will carry a line of O'Donnell watches. That's why I'm here in Danfield—to learn more about Andrew. I like to get acquainted with potential business partners on a personal basis. Ah, here comes my daughter. Joanna is my vice president in charge of personnel. I never go anywhere without her.'

Andrew grumbled something under his breath that Kristin didn't catch. Before she could question him, however, Mr. Larcum proudly presented his daughter. Joanna Larcum was a beautiful woman, although she certainly didn't look like the offspring of tidy, precise Mr. Larcum. She seemed to be a person so sure of her appeal she knew she could afford to take chances with her appearance. Her midnight-black hair tumbled halfway down her back, and she wore a baggy dress that slipped down off one shoulder, a style that flattered her more by accident than design.

Joanna surveyed Kristin with open curiosity. 'So you're the mystery woman Andrew's kept hidden away. At last he's given us a chance to meet you, Christine.'

'It's Kristin. Although I don't exactly think of myself as a mystery woman.' She gave Andrew another sharp glance.

'That's just a figure of speech Joanna uses,' Andrew said. 'I'm sure the Larcums will excuse us. They want to circulate, too.' This time he was forceful about steering Kristin toward the next group of party guests.

Mr. Larcum did turn to speak with someone else, but his daughter Joanna wasn't so easily dissuaded. She bobbed along beside Kristin as Andrew tried to whisk her away. The threesome came to a halt.

'I want to hear all the details about how the two of you met,' Joanna said. 'Andrew's been holding out on me—he's been much too secretive for my taste. Go ahead. How *did* you meet him, Christine?'

'Kristin. But there's nothing to tell. I met Andrew when he volunteered to work with my son. That's it.'

'Yep, that's it,' Andrew agreed, his voice too hearty again.

'There has to be a more imaginative version,' Joanna insisted. 'Humor me, Christine. I'm a romantic.' Joanna had one similarity with her father: a keen gaze that seemed determined to probe beneath the surface. She gave the distinct impression that she relished peering into other people's lives, hoping to discover something unsavory—rather like someone prying up rocks to poke around for worms.

'I'm afraid you won't find anything romantic about my dealings with Andrew,' Kristin said dryly. 'He'd be the first to agree with me on that.' She flushed, though, as she and Andrew gazed at each other, and she remembered the touch of his lips on hers.

Joanna Larcum gave both of them a speculative perusal.

'No romance. I find that hard to believe,' Joanna murmured. 'Every couple needs romance.' She brushed her hand against Andrew's arm, as if laying a subtle claim to him. Andrew, meanwhile, wore a beleaguered look that wasn't subtle in the least. He gave Kristin no chance to ask what this 'couple' business was about. Taking hold of her elbow again, he accelerated away from Joanna Larcum.

'Talk to you later, Joanna,' he said over his shoulder. 'Kristin still hasn't met everybody.'

Apparently Joanna was not to be daunted. She didn't chase after them, but her voice followed them across the room. 'Oh, by the way,' she called. 'Andrew—Christine. Congratulations on your engagement. I forgot to ask if you've set the wedding date!'

Kristin stopped so suddenly that a caterer bearing a plate of hors d'oeuvres almost careened into her. She stared at Andrew in shock.

'Engagement?' she said. '*Wedding* date?'

Andrew didn't seem to be listening. No longer on the move, he simply stood there in the middle of the floor with Kristin, the party eddying around them. He shook his head, as if in disgust.

'Now I'm in it,' he muttered. 'Now I'm really in it.'

172

Kristin tossed down the damp rag she'd been using to wipe the windows. She sank into one of the porch chairs, feeling rather like a damp rag herself. Between motherhood and her veterinary practice, housework didn't stand a chance. Usually she'd wait until she simply couldn't tolerate the clutter anymore, and then she'd dig in with a vengeance. This had been one of her infrequent afternoons of deep-down cleaning. For a few hours it had been therapeutic to sweep and polish and scrub. Certainly it had been a good way to take out some of her frustrations in regard to Andrew O'Donnell, but she could no longer fight the heat of the day. Sherlock was sprawled in an ungainly pile at her feet. He'd recently been groomed, his long fur clipped short, and he looked a bit silly with a green bow tied behind his ears. Kristin petted him, then leaned back in her chair and pressed a half-empty glass of iced tea against her forehead. Not cool enough. She fished some ice cubes out of her glass and popped them down the front of her T-shirt.

The sheepdog lifted his beribboned head as a red Bronco pulled into the drive. A moment later Andrew came striding up the walk. He looked fresh and vibrant, as if he thrived on hot summer sunshine. Kristin watched him as he stopped at the bottom of the porch steps.

'It's no use coming here, Andrew. I don't

want to talk to you. After your party the other night, I think we've both had enough of each other.'

His expression was determined. 'You hang up the phone every time I call. You won't let me explain anything, and you won't even let me see Randy. We have to straighten this out.'

'We don't have to straighten anything out,' she said. 'As far as I'm concerned, you're no longer part of Randy's life. Your forty hours are almost up, anyway. No sense in prolonging the agony. I'm reviewing applications from the community center so someone else can take over the job.'

'What does Randy say about all this?'

Kristin set her glass down on the table. 'Randy's just fine.'

'At least let me talk to him.'

'He's at his swimming class, and I don't expect him back for quite a while. Besides, I've told him what's going on. He understands the situation.'

Andrew propped his arm against the porch railing. 'Exactly what did you tell him? Exactly what *is* the almighty situation here?'

Kristin hesitated. The last day or so with Randy hadn't been pleasant. He'd either moped or grown rowdy, asking about Andrew an average of every ten minutes. But Kristin didn't want Andrew to know any of this.

'I told Randy that it's not easy to find just the right substitute father, and that we were going to look around some more.'

'He's okay with that?'

'He'll *be* okay. Don't worry, Andrew. I didn't tell him anything bad about you. I didn't tell him how you go around announcing to everybody that we're engaged!' Kristin stood and moved to the top of the porch steps. It was hard to be dignified in her baggy T-shirt and denim cutoffs, but she made the attempt. Unfortunately, one of the ice cubes she'd dropped down the front of her T-shirt hadn't melted yet, and now it slipped out the bottom, landing with a *plink* on the steps. Andrew surveyed the ice quizzically, watching it begin to puddle in the sun.

'You think it's right to make Randy suffer just because of ... a little misunderstanding?' he asked.

'Maybe you call it a little misunderstanding,' Kristin said. 'I happen to call it outright deception. I just can't figure out why you'd do it. Why would you go to all the trouble of telling people we're engaged to be married?'

Andrew came up a step. 'That's why I've been calling you. I've been wanting to explain, only you wouldn't let me.'

She didn't care to hear any of his explanations. 'I'm angry at you—and I don't want you around Randy. I mean, how can I let you around him if you have this tendency to concoct stories—'

'You'd understand if you'd just let me get a

word in. Kristin, are you going to hear me out?'

She studied him from her vantage point at the top of the steps. The problem was that Andrew O'Donnell looked so sincere. He had the demeanor of a man who should be trusted—but how could she possibly trust him after the stunt he'd pulled?

'It won't cost you anything to listen,' he said. 'It's only fair that you let me tell my side.'

Kristin deliberated, then turned and banged open the screen door. 'I'll be back,' she said. 'Wait right there for me.'

She went to the kitchen and poured two tall glasses of tea, putting in plenty of ice. She carried them to the porch and thrust one at Andrew. 'Drink,' she said. 'And talk.' She plunked herself down on the steps. 'One more thing,' she added. 'Whatever you have to tell me, it'd better be pretty damn good!'

Now that Kristin had actually given Andrew the go-ahead, he didn't seem to know where to start. He jiggled his glass and scowled down into his tea.

'It's a long story …'

'So you've mentioned before,' Kristin said. 'Why not give me the abridged version?'

Andrew didn't acknowledge the sarcasm in her tone, but simply went on jiggling his glass. The afternoon seemed to grow warmer still. Kristin fished in her own glass for an ice cube and unabashedly popped it down the front of her T-shirt. Andrew watched this with an unreadable expression, and finally he seemed inspired to speak.

'As you're obviously aware, Kristin, lately I've had a run of bad luck where women are concerned. A very bad run. Terrible, I guess you could say.'

Kristin didn't like the way he'd phrased that. 'Correction, Andrew. It'd be far more accurate to say that women have had a run of bad luck with *you*.'

He gave her a quelling look. 'You'll have plenty of chance to get your gibes in later. Just listen to me. Like I said, things haven't worked out for me with women lately. It all comes down to a difference of opinion, actually.'

'Right, right. Those women you date want love and marriage and commitment. You don't.' Kristin popped another ice cube down her T-shirt. Andrew studied her almost reproachfully.

'That's damn distracting, what you're doing with that ice,' he pointed out.

'I'm just trying to deal with the heat any way I can.'

'It's still distracting me,' he objected.

She crossed her arms in front of her T-shirt, frowning at him. 'You were saying, Andrew?'

He took a good swallow of tea, growing contemplative now. 'After dating the Honorable Loraine Thaxter, I decided to give myself a breather from women. But it's not easy to take a breather when every woman in the vicinity knows you're unattached and when you have a reputation as a bit of a ... hmm, man about town.' For a moment he wore a wry expression, as if considering whether his choice of words was appropriate. Then he shrugged and went on.

'I did find a solution, however,' he said. 'One day, when I was being pressed by a particularly gregarious brunette who works for me, I happened to imply that I was attached. Engaged, to be exact. It was amazing how fast that did the trick. She lost interest right away. It was also amazing how fast news of this sort travels in a company like mine. The implication turned into a rumor. And then the rumor turned into something my employees took as established fact.'

Kristin was impressed by the peculiar twists of Andrew's imagination. 'Amazing, truly amazing,' she murmured.

'Hey, at least it did the job,' he defended himself. 'That one little hint, and before I knew it I had my breather.'

Kristin gazed at him skeptically. 'Am I supposed to congratulate you for being devious?'

'It didn't seem devious at the time. It seemed more like an act of self-preservation. And it sure was convenient for a while there. I had all the peace I needed to work on expanding my business.'

Now Andrew's face took on the intense look

it always did when he discussed his great-grandfather's company. 'I put a lot of effort into convincing Benjamin Larcum he should come to Danfield and check out my timepieces. If he decides to carry my watches in his stores, it'll be the opportunity I've been looking for. Other accounts will follow, and my gamble with O'Donnell's Fine Timepieces will pay off. I'll be able to go somewhere with the company.'

For a moment Andrew seemed lost in his vision of the future, but then he stared morosely into his tea again. 'Damn,' he said. 'The only thing I didn't count on in all this was Joanna Larcum.'

Kristin was actually beginning to enjoy their little chat. She leaned back on the steps, sipping her tea. 'It's all becoming clear,' she said solemnly. 'Joanna showed a bit too much interest in you, and you fed her your line about being engaged. Only she wasn't so easily put off. She was too smart to believe you. She wanted proof.'

Andrew held up his hand. 'Don't get ahead of things. It didn't happen like that. Mr. Larcum was the one who heard the rumor about me being engaged. When he congratulated me, I never got around to scotching any misconceptions he had.' Andrew sounded like a man who'd dug a deeper and deeper hole for himself and had no idea how to climb out. 'Hell, Mr. Larcum seemed to approve of my alleged engagement so thoroughly, and I already had so much riding on this contract with his department stores ... Besides, it didn't hurt to have Joanna Larcum think I was engaged, too. She was circling me like a shark at feeding time. This makes you laugh, Kristin? You find this amusing?'

Kristin shook her head, confounded at the amount of trouble Andrew O'Donnell could stir up. 'A plan like yours always comes to a downfall. And your downfall happens to be Joanna Larcum. I suppose I *do* see a certain pleasing humor in that. Something tells me Joanna is going to tear you apart when she finds out the truth. Shark bait is right.'

'You haven't heard the whole story,' Andrew went on gloomily. 'When Mr. Larcum saw you and me together the other day at my office, he just went ahead and assumed you were my fiancée.'

Suddenly Kristin wasn't quite so amused anymore. 'Of course you didn't bother to scotch this misconception, either.'

'I'd gotten myself in too deep at that point. I'd already arranged the cocktail party for Mr. Larcum to meet my employees, and he expected me to introduce my fiancée—the new vet in town. And Joanna kept pressing to meet my fiancée, too. Any way I looked at it, I needed you to show up at that party with me.'

Kristin was sorely tempted to dump her iced tea on Andrew's head. 'In all these gyrations of yours, you forgot one little detail—namely, letting me in on the secret. At least you could have told me I was supposed to be masquerading as your soon-to-be.'

Andrew didn't show the remorse she would have liked. 'I had every intention of explaining my predicament to you,' he said. 'I was going to ask for your cooperation ahead of time. But when I called to tell you about the party, you acted like it was a major act of war that I'd even think of inviting you.'

'That's no excuse,' she protested.

'Would you have agreed to the party if I'd asked you to pretend to be my fiancée?' He made it sound as if he was posing a perfectly reasonable question.

'Of course I wouldn't have agreed,' Kristin said. 'I would've slammed the phone in your ear.'

'You slammed it in my ear, anyway, remember? So I figured I'd get you to the party and then I'd explain. Only the right moment never seemed to come along.'

'So that's why you shuttled me so fast from one guest to the next,' Kristin said, marveling anew at Andrew's scheme. 'You were hoping no one would say the wrong thing to me. Your secretary almost *did* say the wrong thing, but you managed to get away from her in time. Of course, once again, you didn't count on Joanna Larcum.'

Andrew grimaced. 'Who can predict what a

woman like Joanna will do? Look, I'm the first to admit I got myself into one heck of a pickle. I'm starting to wish I'd never heard the word "engagement." Maybe you can see that what I'm trying to do here is apologize.'

Kristin wrapped her arms around her knees and gazed at him. He looked sorry, indeed. 'I never turn down an apology, Andrew. Even one as convoluted as yours.'

Andrew nodded, then barreled on as if the situation was entirely solved. 'Good. I promised Randy I'd take him to the zoo this Saturday. I wouldn't want to let him down.'

'Hold on,' Kristin said. 'Accepting your apology is one thing. Letting you go on volunteering with Randy is something else again. Randy needs someone he can trust. Someone *I* can trust. But how am I supposed to do that now?'

'It's simple,' Andrew said quietly. 'I made a mistake, I acknowledged the mistake. We go on from there. At least let me finish my forty hours with Randy. I owe him that much.'

Kristin stood and pushed away the wisps of hair that had straggled onto her forehead. 'We don't go on,' she said, wondering why it was so difficult to say those words. 'Andrew, everything that happened with my ex-husband taught me that I can't afford mistakes where Randy's concerned. After this engagement fracas of yours, how do I know what you'll do next?'

'I'm not your ex-husband. And I don't jump from one fracas to the next.'

'How can I know that?' she said stubbornly. 'I just can't take the chance. I don't want you part of Randy's life anymore.'

Nothing remained to be said, it seemed. His face carefully devoid of expression, Andrew reached over to her and handed back his glass of iced tea. A breeze rustled the leaves of the weeping willow in the yard, creating a mournful sound. Andrew began to go down the steps. But then he turned back to Kristin.

'You keep saying you're trying to protect Randy, but you're not really being truthful. You're trying to protect yourself, more than anything else. And if you're not careful ... you might be the one who ends up hurting Randy.'

'I would never hurt my son!'

'Not intentionally, anyway.' And with that he left her. A moment later he drove away from her house, gravel flying up from under his wheels.

Kristin grabbed her cleaning rag and attacked the windows again. Andrew was wrong. Just now she'd done the best thing for Randy, the only thing she *could* do. In the long run, it would be better for Randy to have another substitute dad. She was being a good parent, that was all.

So why did she feel so downright miserable about it?

CHAPTER SIX

'All young lovers have tiffs, Dr. Mabry. It's to be expected. But I was beginning to worry that you and Andrew wouldn't patch things up, after all. I'm so glad you came here to see him today.' Andrew O'Donnell's secretary, Ginnie, smiled benevolently at Kristin. At the moment, Kristin was sitting across from Ginnie's desk at O'Donnell's Fine Timepieces. Ginnie's manner was warm and down to earth, yet everything she said made Kristin want to holler. She hardly knew where to begin to correct Ginnie's misconceptions. Obviously the woman still believed Kristin was Andrew's fiancée.

'Andrew's out back at the loading dock,' Ginnie said. 'I'll page him and have him here for you right away. I can't wait to see the two of you together again.' Seconds later Ginnie was talking to her boss on the phone. 'Yes, Andrew, your Dr. Mabry is right here, in my office. What do you mean, how does she look? She looks a bit peaked, that's how she looks. Brides-to-be are under a lot of pressure, Andrew. You have to bear that in mind.' Ginnie hung up and gave Kristin a consoling glance. 'Don't worry, dear, he's on his way. The two of you will have your troubles straightened out in no time.'

Kristin made a sound that was somewhere between a laugh and a moan. What was the use of trying to explain this snarl, anyway? It had been a week since Kristin had last seen Andrew, a week since he'd come to her house to apologize. Somehow it seemed much longer than that, perhaps because Randy had been so difficult to handle these past few days, constantly asking when he could see Andrew again. This afternoon, to distract her son, Kristin had taken him with her to a farm outside town where she'd inspected the dairy herd. Usually such outings enthralled Randy. Today, however, Randy had simply moped, interjecting Andrew's name into the conversation at every opportunity. It was amazing how relentless an eight-year-old child could be. When Kristin had returned to town, she'd dropped Randy off at Pam's house. Then she'd come straight to O'Donnell's.

Now Andrew appeared at the door to Ginnie's office and surveyed Kristin. 'I didn't expect to see you here,' he said, sounding reserved, and Kristin immediately sensed the distance in his manner.

She stood. 'Andrew, we have to talk. I know you're probably quite busy, but—'

'Matter of fact, I am busy.'

He refused to make this easy for her, that much was obvious. But Ginnie intervened.

'Andrew, you know I can manage everything on my own for a few minutes. Talk to Dr. Mabry. Work things out.'

Andrew gave his secretary a sardonic glance. 'Yes, I know you can manage everything, Ginnie—including me.'

'Someone has to manage you,' she said tartly. 'Go on, the two of you!'

Andrew hesitated another moment, then gave Kristin a brusque nod. 'I'm on my way up to see one of my foremen. Come along, if you like.' He turned and strode toward an elevator at the back of the showroom, and Kristin had to hurry to catch up. He was making it clear this encounter would be on his terms, not hers. For the moment she had no choice but to follow.

The elevator took them to one of the upper floors, and Kristin emerged into an intriguing world of machinery. She glanced around as Andrew went off to speak to his foreman. Different workstations had been arranged in the well-lit room. At one station, Kristin saw a woman operating a machine that had a complex array of wire baskets and glass tubes. At another station, a man wearing an eye loupe turned a delicate screwdriver on a watch, reminding Kristin of a surgeon bending over his patient with a scalpel. Everything about this place seemed to be ordered on a small, intimate scale. Craftsmanship was the word that came immediately to Kristin's mind, an old-style craftsmanship where watchmakers took pride in their skills. This was no

186

impersonal assembly line.

Kristin noticed something else. None of the workers seemed to tense up with Andrew around. Business simply proceeded at a relaxed yet steady pace. Obviously these employees were comfortable with Andrew. Kristin had already learned that many workers had been with O'Donnell's Fine Timepieces for years, even decades. Once more, Kristin gained a sense of the continuity in Andrew's life, the traditions he respected and nurtured by revitalizing this family business of his.

Andrew finished his discussion with the foreman and returned to Kristin. He glanced at his watch. 'Time for you to have your say. Come on, you can talk while I eat something. Didn't get much of a lunch earlier.' Andrew sounded brisk, again making it clear that she was an intrusion on his schedule.

He led her to the elevator and up to the third floor, then escorted her into an area that obviously served as a lunch-room. Opening the door of a large refrigerator, he helped himself to a sandwich from a tray.

'Have something to eat yourself,' he said.

Come to think of it, she hadn't stopped for much of a lunch, either. The array of food was enticing: not only trays of fresh sandwiches, but bowls of tossed salad, several varieties of fruit and a selection of desserts. Kristin gave herself a slice of melon and a large, whole-wheat cinnamon roll. As she sat down at one of the tables with Andrew, she smiled tentatively at him.

'I'm impressed with the way you run this place,' she said. 'A person could be very happy working here. You've thought of everything, right down to the snacks. This cinnamon roll tastes homemade.'

He regarded her over his sandwich. 'Something tells me you didn't come here to admire my managerial abilities. Out with it, Kristin. What's on your mind?'

Now that the moment had come, she was reluctant to begin.

'I'm here ... I'm here because ... darn it, I have to ask you a favor!'

'A favor. I see.' Andrew's expression remained noncommittal, and he devoted himself to his turkey-and-sprout sandwich.

Kristin speared a chunk of melon with her fork, but then frowned at her plate without eating. 'Yes, well, it's simple, really. The truth is, I'd like to ... reinstate you. As Randy's volunteer dad, that is. I—he needs you. I want to do what's best for my son. And you, Andrew ... somehow you seem to be what's best.'

'Hmm. Now I'm what's best for your son. You sure didn't think so last week. What changed your mind?'

This was humiliating, it truly was. 'Randy's been sad without you. Nothing seems to cheer him up. Even when I tried another substitute father—'

'Another substitute? You're really something, Kristin. You act like a dad for Randy is a mail-order item. If one doesn't work out, hey, send it back and request another one.'

'I don't see why you're getting so worked up,' she said. 'You never wanted the job in the first place. And the whole point of this volunteer program was to give Randy and me a number of choices. The whole point was not to depend too much on any one person! But it hasn't worked out the way I expected—not since *you* showed up on my porch, anyway.'

Andrew clasped his hands behind his head, apparently no longer in a hurry. The sun slanting through the blinds cast a barred pattern across the table and across Andrew's features. That made it difficult to gauge his mood, but she sensed a subtle shift of attitude in him. It made her wary.

'Sure miffs you, doesn't it?' he asked. 'Finding out I'm your only choice, after all. Having to show up here and ask me to come back. Admitting that maybe you were wrong about me.'

'There's no need to rub it in,' she said. 'I *am* apologizing.'

'Are you willing to bargain with me, Kristin?'

She became even more wary. 'I don't know what you mean.'

'Just what I said. We'll make a bargain. I'll

189

come back and finish up my forty hours as Randy's substitute dad. No. I'll do better than that. I'll agree to an additional forty hours—if you'll do something for me. As it turns out, I still need a fiancée—a substitute fiancée, that is. And you're elected for the job.'

She couldn't believe what he was saying. 'Oh, no. Not this all over again! Are you crazy, Andrew?'

'Just pragmatic. This deal with the Larcums could make or break O'Donnell's. Mr. Larcum keeps asking about you, and so does Joanna. I didn't count on having a fiancée who'd invite so much curiosity. It's damn inconvenient, but there it is.'

Kristin had completely lost her appetite. Her cinnamon roll might just as well have been sawdust, and she pushed it away. 'Are you telling me the Larcums still think we're engaged? Well, you can go right out and tell them we've become *disengaged*.'

'Afraid I can't do that,' Andrew said. He pushed his own plate away, seeming to have lost his appetite, too. 'This weekend there's a grand opening for a Larcum store in Oklahoma City. That's one of the reasons I was able to get Mr. Larcum to visit O'Donnell's Fine Timepieces—I told him he could just schedule a trip to Danfield along with the festivities for his new store. But there's a slight hitch. Mr. Larcum expects me to attend the opening with my one and only. In other words, he expects me to show up with you.'

'Forget it!' she exclaimed. 'Nothing doing. Never. Nix—'

'It's part of the deal. One substitute fiancée in exchange for one substitute dad.'

Kristin gazed across the table at Andrew. Before today, she'd almost come to believe that he possessed certain qualities worthy of approval. After all, she admired the vision he had for his great-grandfather's company and the way he'd risked everything to make that vision come true. Also, children and animals took to the man right away. That was definitely a point in his favor. But now Andrew was challenging those favorable opinions.

'I can't believe you'd be this callous,' she said. 'A little boy's happiness is at stake, and you're using it for leverage.'

'Yes, it is callous of me, isn't it? Kind of like how you booted me out, then crooked your finger because I could still be of use. But don't worry, Kristin. I'll come back. Only thing is, this reinstatement business doesn't come cheap.'

Kristin knew what she ought to do right now. She ought to stand up, march out of the building and never return. Hadn't Andrew just proved he was no role model for her son? Counterfeit engagements, bogus fiancées— and obnoxious bargains in the process. Was this the kind of man she wanted as a role model for her son?

But then Kristin remembered the sad look Randy had been wearing. She wanted to see him happy again. More than anything, that was what she wanted.

'Let me get this straight,' she said. 'I show up with you in Oklahoma City, pretending to be your fiancée—'

'My adoring fiancée,' Andrew interjected, poker-faced.

'Don't press your luck,' she muttered. 'Let's be very clear. I show up for this one event as your so-called intended, and you'll volunteer with Randy again. You'll even put in an additional forty hours. That's it? End of story?'

'Right. It's a one-time shot. You go to the store opening with me, do your part and that's it. After that, you can count on me to fulfill my end of the bargain.'

Kristin wondered how she'd come to this disgraceful pass. Today she'd decided that any amount of time her son could be with Andrew O'Donnell was better than nothing at all. But in order to have Andrew spend a few more hours with Randy, she'd have to subject herself to a ridiculous charade.

'I'll do it,' she said grudgingly. 'I'll go to the opening with you, but don't expect me to be happy about it.'

'Fair enough.' He held out his hand to her. 'Shake on the deal?'

Kristin glared at him. But after a long moment she stuck out her hand. 'Shake,' she said tersely.

He clasped her hand across the table and didn't let go. 'I think I could start to enjoy being engaged, as long as it's on a temporary basis like this. Maybe you'll start to enjoy yourself, too, Kristin.'

He moved his fingers over hers, his touch enticing. Then, she detected the humor playing across his features. Snatching her hand away, she pushed back her chair.

'Goodbye, Andrew.'

She was almost out the door when he called to her. 'Kristin—wait.'

She turned and saw that his expression was completely serious.

'I think there's something I should tell you,' he said. 'Even if you hadn't agreed to your half of the bargain, I would've come back. I would've signed on for the extra forty hours, as well.'

She stared at Andrew. 'You put me through all this for nothing?' she demanded.

'No, not for nothing,' he said, still serious. 'I'm in a pickle with this fiancée business. I need your help, and I admit I used a little coercion to get it.'

'Of all the rotten—'

'We shook on the deal,' he reminded her. 'No going back.'

Unfortunately, Kristin never reneged on her promises—not even a promise as bizarre as this one. Like it or not, she was going to be

Andrew's substitute fiancée.

*　　　*　　　*

'Let's cruise on over to the jewelry department, honey. We have to get you an engagement ring, and fast.'

'Andrew, will you stop calling me that? I'm *not* your honey.' The words were out before Kristin realized how ridiculous they sounded. This whole situation was ridiculous. She and Andrew had been at the grand opening of the new Larcum store for barely an hour, and already Kristin felt as if she were going to unravel from the strain of portraying a bride-to-be.

Now Andrew clasped her hand and drew her across the marbled floor. 'Something tells me you're not getting into the spirit of our venture,' he said.

'I think I've done an excellent job so far,' she protested. 'At the ribbon-cutting ceremony, Mr. Larcum seemed quite convinced that you'd shown up with a genuine fiancée.'

'Yes, but I can tell Joanna's starting to get skeptical.'

It had been awkward, indeed, when Joanna Larcum pointed out that Kristin wasn't wearing an engagement ring. But Kristin didn't think it was necessary to get carried away. She did *not* want to visit the jewelry department, feeling no need to indulge

194

Andrew's perverse sense of humor. Why was he enjoying himself so much?

She tried to resist Andrew, but he inexorably propelled her forward. The Larcum department store was the expensive, tasteful sort of place where she felt she ought to walk very softly and speak in hushed tones. Cut-glass vases and brass lamps gleamed on crystal tables; here and there trays of filigreed silver and gilded candelabra were displayed like so many museum pieces. When Kristin and Andrew reached the jewelry department, she was so tense she gripped Andrew's fingers.

'You've got some strength in your muscles there,' he observed.

'It comes from grappling with animals who don't want their shots. I always win the tussle.' Kristin didn't know why she was holding on to Andrew as if he were a lifeline. He was the one who'd gotten her into this mess, after all. 'I hate subterfuge,' she grumbled. 'It's not in my nature.'

'It's not in mine, either. I never intended for my engagement to mushroom like this,' he said. 'Trust me—after the Larcums leave Oklahoma, I'm never getting engaged again. By the way, what kind of ring would you like? They have plenty to choose from here.'

'Andrew, we're not actually going to buy a ring. Let Joanna Larcum think what she likes.'

Andrew didn't pay any attention. He asked a chic saleslady to show him engagement rings, and in a matter of minutes several were laid out before Kristin, the diamonds sparkling up at her from a black velvet cloth.

'I refuse to do something this absurd.'

'Honey, just try this one on for size.' Andrew smiled at Kristin and then at the saleslady, as if to imply that his fiancée was a tad recalcitrant but would come around in the end.

Kristin rolled her eyes, but before she knew it Andrew had slipped a ring onto her left hand. She had to admit he'd made an attractive choice: a small stone surrounded by a delicate swirl of gold. She wiggled her finger experimentally. She hadn't bothered with rings of any type since she'd taken off her wedding band. And, quite frankly, she'd never expected to see a ring on this finger again. It felt odd to wear one for even a second or two.

'It suits you,' Andrew said in a reflective voice. 'It's not the kind of ring that'd get in the way. You could go about your business as usual, tussling with those animals who don't want their shots.'

Somehow she could picture herself living with this ring, glancing at it now and then, and being a little surprised to see it on her finger. Surprised, but maybe pleased, too . . .

Quickly she pulled it off and set it back on the velvet. 'No ring,' she said.

The saleslady looked disappointed—and, oddly enough, so did Andrew. He glanced around.

'Could be my watches will be displayed here soon,' he said. 'It all depends on whether or not I can convince Mr. Larcum to sign that contract.'

'For what it's worth, I hope you get the contract, Andrew. Your watches, at least, are sincere. Old-fashioned and elegant.'

He propped his elbow on the counter. 'You approve of my timepieces, anyway. That's something. But it was my great-grandfather who set the standard. He was one of the original eighty-niners—made the land run with all the other boomers who crowded in here when the territory opened up.'

As always, Kristin was drawn by the appeal of Andrew's heritage. She rested her own elbow on the counter and studied him. His expression was pensive.

'Great-Grandpa came rattling into Danfield in a wagon about to fall to pieces,' he said. 'Didn't have so much as pocket change, but he sure knew what made a watch tick. I envy him sometimes, the chance he had to see one of the last frontiers. I think maybe I was born in the wrong era. Should've been a pioneer myself, fighting to stake out my claim.'

'You've staked your own claim in Oklahoma,' Kristin murmured. 'This is where you belong.'

Now Andrew was the one who studied Kristin, a thoughtful frown etching his features. She wondered what he could be thinking and wished he'd just go on talking about his great-grandfather. There was something comforting about that long-ago world, where emotions had all been played out.

'You two are cozy,' came Joanna's voice from behind Kristin. 'I wondered where you'd disappeared to.'

Kristin turned and gave Joanna Larcum a less than welcoming glance. Today Joanna wore a turtleneck dress that was saved from dowdiness by a colorful belt cinched at the waist. Yet somehow the dress suited her, its very lack of style highlighting the woman's beauty.

'Are you both having a good time?' Joanna asked, her gaze flickering over the diamonds still spread out on velvet. 'Dear me, looks like I've interrupted something ... meaningful.' Nevertheless, she didn't seem to mind interrupting. She sauntered over to Andrew and stood a bit too close to him at the jewelry counter.

Kristin began to feel more involved in her role. She was supposed to portray a fiancée; very well, she'd *act* like a fiancée. She nudged her way between Andrew and Joanna, then gazed raptly at the diamonds glittering before her.

'Andrew and I were just choosing a ring,' she said, tucking her hand around his arm. 'Weren't we, honey?'

He had the grace not to look startled, and

only the slightest twitch of his mouth betrayed amusement. 'That's right . . . honey. We've had such a whirlwind courtship that we haven't taken care of the basics yet. Rings, wedding dates, all that stuff.'

'A whirlwind courtship,' Joanna echoed. 'So the two of you haven't known each other long.'

'Sometimes love hits a person fast,' Kristin improvised. 'It barrels right over you, in fact.' She picked up the ring Andrew had chosen a few moments ago and slipped it back on her finger. 'What do you think, Joanna? Andrew likes this one.'

Joanna wore a disgruntled look. 'I'm sure you'll be satisfied with any item at Larcum.' She turned to the saleslady, who'd come bustling over again. 'Estelle, please open an account in Mr. O'Donnell's name. It appears he'll be purchasing this ring for Dr. Mabry.'

Kristin automatically opened her mouth to protest, then clamped it shut again without saying anything. She could hardly blame Andrew or anyone else for getting her into this mess. She'd done all the work on her own.

Andrew slipped his arm around her shoulders and gave her a squeeze. 'Darling, looks like you've got yourself an engagement ring. How does it feel?'

'Oh . . . just dandy.'

'Congratulations,' Joanna said stiffly. 'If you'll excuse me, I need to see how our other customers are faring. Opening day is always hectic.' She began to walk away, then paused and turned to stare at Andrew and Kristin.

Andrew tilted Kristin's chin. 'Darling,' he repeated, loud enough that Joanna would be sure to overhear. Then he smiled at Kristin and gave her a kiss, right there in full view of the saleslady and Joanna Larcum.

It was a persuasive kiss—so persuasive, in fact, that Kristin forgot about her audience, forgot her own subterfuge, forgot altogether that she was playing a role. She was aware only of Andrew's mouth on hers, the taste of his lips—and the way he drew her close as if to make sure the kiss wouldn't end anytime soon.

CHAPTER SEVEN

Unfortunately, all good kisses must come to an end. When *this* kiss ended, Kristin found her hands on Andrew's shoulders, the diamond on her finger giving off a cheerful glint and seeming to mock her. Perhaps she was a counterfeit fiancée, but that had been no counterfeit kiss. She gazed at Andrew, her lips still parted breathlessly. He gazed back, looking just a bit puzzled himself, as if he hadn't expected the kiss to be quite so believable, either.

'Well,' said Joanna Larcum. 'Well!' She sped away, glancing over her shoulder one more time.

Kristin stepped back from Andrew, not sure what to do next. Perhaps it was best not to do anything at all. Hadn't she already got herself into enough of a fix?

Andrew filled out some paperwork at the counter, signing his name forcefully. Afterward the saleslady handed him a ring box to take along, and she gave a misty-eyed smile to both Kristin and Andrew.

'I can tell how much you care for each other,' she said. 'Congratulations—and have a wonderful life together.'

Kristin almost groaned out loud. She pulled Andrew away from the jewelry counter. 'Now we've done it,' she said. 'Was that kiss really necessary? And you just bought me an engagement ring!'

'Looks like it, doesn't it?' He didn't seem overly perturbed.

'Would you take this seriously?' she demanded. 'Next thing we know, we'll have the date set at the wedding chapel, and then all of a sudden we'll be picking rice out of our hair.'

'This engagement does have a way of getting out of hand,' he acknowledged. 'It seems to take on a life all its own.'

Andrew still didn't seem properly concerned. Kristin hauled him off to a more secluded area of the store. In the women's clothing section, she spied some chairs angled against the wall and headed toward them.

Maybe she could think better sitting down.

She plopped into one of the chairs and spread her left hand out on her skirt. She stared at her ring finger as if it belonged to someone else entirely. 'What on earth are we going to do with this diamond?' she asked.

'Guess you'll just have to wear it for the time being.' Andrew sat in a chair beside her and stretched out his legs. 'Relax, Kristin. Everything's going according to plan.'

'Plan—what plan? Andrew, the problem with you is that you don't *have* a plan. You just threw the two of us into this headfirst, without thinking it through.'

'I keep trying to tell you I don't have a devious mind. I'm just trying to climb out of this stew I made for myself.'

It felt like a stew, all right, a big pot of stew with far too many ingredients bubbling around. Kristin slumped back. 'I'll wear the ring today, and then you can return it and have it taken off your account,' she said. 'That's a solution. Except that Joanna will find out about it, sure as anything, and she'll probably get suspicious all over again. We can't have that.'

'You're really starting to get caught up in this,' Andrew said with a note of interest. 'You've captured the spirit of our engagement, after all.'

Andrew was joking. Of course he was joking. Kristin saw the hint of humor in his eyes. So why did she so easily picture actually being engaged to this man, wearing his ring, making all sorts of complicated wedding plans, having him near her always....?

Kristin was appalled at her imagination. She shook her head, as if to dispel these wayward images. 'In case you haven't realized it yet,' she said, 'real engagements aren't part of my agenda. I'm never getting married again—never. One mistake like that was enough for an entire lifetime.'

'It seems when I least expect it, I touch a nerve with you.' Andrew's voice was surprisingly gentle. 'Okay, so this one guy was a real jerk, and you had the bad luck to hook up with him. That doesn't mean that somewhere down the road you won't find someone you could be happy with.'

How easy he made it sound! Kristin shook her head. 'It's not a matter of bad luck or good luck. I *chose* my husband. I was absolutely convinced that I could see him clearly and that marrying him was the right thing to do. It just makes me wonder if I know anything about men at all.' She crossed her arms, as if that would somehow prevent her from confessing more of her fears. This seemed such an unlikely place for confessions: on a chair beside Andrew, surrounded by a thicket of dresses and three-way mirrors.

'If you got married again, you'd be able to provide a real dad for Randy,' he pointed out.

'Maybe that's worth the risk.'

'Much as I love my son, that's the wrong reason for getting married. No. It's better this way.'

'Right,' he said. 'With a substitute father who knows his place, and no other men in your life.'

She gave him a sharp glance. 'I know what's best for Randy and me. We've been through a lot, the two of us. Don't you see, Andrew? I can't risk it again! My ex-husband cast Randy aside to make a fresh start—like throwing out old clothes so he could buy a whole new wardrobe. No little boy should have to go through that more than once.'

Andrew regarded her with a quiet, steady gaze. 'Randy wasn't the only one cast aside, was he? And now you've decided that you'll be the one in charge, showing any man the door before he has a chance to betray you.'

Kristin stood and pulled the diamond off her finger. 'I think this farce of ours has gone on long enough, don't you? We've already played our parts for Mr. Larcum, and for Joanna.' She held the ring out to him, but he didn't take it.

'I guess I touched another nerve,' he said.

'Nerve. *You* have a lot of nerve, Andrew.' She glared at him. 'You're the one who kissed me just now, when it was completely unnecessary. Joanna didn't need that much convincing.'

He rose to stand beside Kristin. 'I like to do a thorough job whatever I'm attempting. I'd say that was a necessary kiss, as opposed to a completely unnecessary one.' Clearly the situation still amused him.

'Dammit, Andrew, that kiss went too far. It felt too real—' She stopped herself, but not in time. She gazed at him, still clutching the diamond ring. And she saw the humor fade from his expression.

'Kristin ... about that kiss ...'

'I don't see why we have to talk about it anymore.' For some reason her heart had begun to pound erratically. If just discussing a kiss could do this to her, she was in bad shape, indeed.

But it seemed Andrew agreed there should be no more talking. He didn't say another word. He simply took Kristin in his arms, and he kissed her again.

With no one watching them this time—no one at all—Andrew kissed her quite thoroughly, there among the gowns of the Larcum department store.

* * *

Kristin balanced the telephone receiver between her ear and shoulder, getting a crick in her neck but leaving her hands free for the bowl of pancake batter she was stirring. She listened as Andrew's voice came over the wire.

'Just go with me one last time, Kristin. That's all I'm asking.'

'Impossible,' she said. 'I can't pretend to be your fiancée again. I thought we finished with all that yesterday at the department store.'

'Hear me out. I'm not asking you to pretend anymore. But the Larcums have invited both you and me to dinner tonight. I think we should go. I'm planning to put everything straight, and I'd like you to be there.'

Kristin jabbed at the batter with her spatula. 'What are you talking about, Andrew?'

His voice revealed no emotion. 'Maybe I've simply decided I'm not cut out for a life of intrigue. I'm going to tell the Larcums the truth about our alleged engagement.'

Kristin wanted to argue. 'I wish you'd thought of that before yesterday. We went to so much trouble. We did such a good job of convincing everyone, after all.'

'Maybe we did too good a job,' he remarked.

Now she cradled the bowl in the curve of her arm and gripped the receiver with her free hand. She understood what Andrew was implying: perhaps they'd done too good a job of convincing themselves. When Andrew had kissed her that second time, there among the gowns...

Afterward Kristin had been trembling, that was all she knew.

'You'll be placing your contract with Mr. Larcum in jeopardy,' she said. 'He probably isn't going to be too pleased to find out the whole engagement was a masquerade. No one likes to feel deceived.'

Now the slightest hint of irony crept into Andrew's tone. 'And I don't like to deceive. That's why it's better this way, even if I lose the contract.'

She couldn't help admiring his scruples, yet a heaviness had settled inside her. 'Too bad all our good acting abilities will go for nothing,' she tried to joke. 'We had everything covered, even the engagement ring.' Last night, for safekeeping, she'd tucked the diamond into one of her bureau drawers after wrapping it carefully in a lace handkerchief. She didn't understand why she hadn't simply returned the ring to Andrew ...

'So you'll come with me, Kristin?' he asked. 'I figure it's only fair that you hear my explanation to the Larcums.'

Why did she feel so melancholy? As if she was mourning an engagement that had truly existed? 'All right, I'll go to dinner with you,' she murmured.

'I'm still taking Randy to that softball game this afternoon.'

'He's looking forward to it.' Kristin's voice softened at the mention of her son. 'Randy can't wait to see you again.'

'Talk to you later, then.'

'Yes ... later.' Kristin slowly replaced the receiver and stood for a moment, halfheartedly poking her spatula at the pancake batter. When she turned around, she saw her son standing in the doorway from the hall. He was still in his rumpled pajamas, but he looked alert and wide awake. Randy was always ready to go from the second he opened his eyes in the morning.

'Hi there, pal,' Kristin said. 'Hungry for breakfast? It's pancakes this time, and blueberry syrup.' During the week they too often rushed through their meals, but Kristin made sure that Sunday mornings, at least, were leisurely.

Randy wandered into the kitchen. 'What time is Andrew coming, Mom?'

'Right after lunch. He's missed you. And you should know...' Kristin hesitated. 'Well, you should know he didn't stay away because he wanted to.'

'Sure, I get it. He stayed away because you were mad at him.'

'Something like that,' she said ruefully. She watched as her son climbed onto a chair and dragged the jar of syrup out of the cupboard. Whenever Randy was around, the house seemed to fill up with motion and life. He was still poking through the cupboard like an explorer on a science mission.

'How about pickle relish on pancakes? You ever try that, Mom?'

'Not a chance.' She spooned batter onto the grill.

'Catsup on pancakes?'

'Even less of a chance.'

'Mom, are you gonna marry Andrew?'

Kristin almost flipped her bowl of batter onto the floor. It was a moment before she trusted herself to speak in a normal tone of voice. She gazed at her son. 'Me ... marry Andrew? Whatever gave you that idea?'

'You always whisper to him on the phone and you go on dates. And Jonah's mom says you're gonna get married.'

Pam, unfortunately, must finally have heard the rumors about Kristin's 'engagement.' Kristin piled some pancakes onto a plate for Randy and waited for him to start in on them. Then she sat down too.

'Randy ... I'm not going to marry Andrew.'

'But if you married him, he'd be my real dad,' Randy said stubbornly. 'Jonah has a real dad.'

At that moment Holmes the cat went streaking through the kitchen, followed a second later by Sherlock the sheepdog. The two of them made a mad dash around the table, then careered out of the room again.

'You see?' Kristin said. 'We're a real family right now, all of us—you, me, Holmes, Sherlock, Watson and Hercule Poirot.'

She was rewarded with just the smallest, blueberry-tinged smile. 'Don't forget Agatha and Christie,' Randy said.

Kristin's heart ached for her son. She wished

she could wave a magic wand and give him the type of family he longed for—the type of family he'd never really known. A husband and wife who loved one another, and who both loved their son. Now she realized how dangerous it had been to indulge in that so-called engagement with Andrew. The rumors about it had already stirred Randy's hopes. Kristin was determined to straighten out this whole engagement fiasco before something even worse happened.

Andrew was right. It was best not to pretend any longer.

* * *

The Sequoyah Hotel in Danfield was an elegant, stately establishment. Sateen draperies hung at the tall windows of the lobby, and thick carpeting in an arabesque design covered the floor. Kristin's heels sank into the carpet, her footsteps silent as she crossed the lobby at Andrew's side.

'Nervous?' he asked.

'A little, I suppose.'

'Don't worry, I'll handle everything. You can just sit back and enjoy the meal. I'm the one who got us both into this jam with the Larcums, and I'll get us out.'

Kristin smoothed the collar of her crepe jacket. She'd taken particular care with her appearance tonight, wearing this creamy blazer over a soft paisley dress. She'd also swept her hair up off her neck. This might be her last appearance as Andrew's fiancée, but she was determined to look her best.

'You know, I take *some* responsibility for this predicament we're in,' she said. 'I can handle my end of it.' She glanced over at him, struck by how handsome he looked tonight. He'd dressed more formally than usual, in a suit of heathery tan and a dark silk tie, as if he, too, needed to appear his best for the difficult task ahead.

Mr. Larcum and his daughter were already waiting in the hotel restaurant. Mr. Larcum seemed happy and genial, but Joanna behaved in reserved fashion toward Andrew and Kristin. By the time the four of them had settled at a table with pre-dinner drinks, the conversation began to lag a bit. Joanna sipped her lime tonic and gazed pointedly at Kristin's left hand. No doubt Joanna was noting the lack of an engagement ring. The diamond Andrew had purchased was still inside Kristin's bureau drawer at home.

'Mr. Larcum,' Kristin said rather forcefully. 'How are you enjoying your visit to Danfield?'

'It's a tolerable place, Dr. Mabry. Tolerable.' Mr. Larcum, tidy and spruce as always, shook his napkin as if on the lookout for renegade crumbs. 'Andrew has been filling me in on the local history. I've been most interested to learn about the Oklahoma land

211

run in 1889. Andrew tells me Danfield became a town overnight, when thousands of settlers poured in here to stake their claims.'

Joanna Larcum finally showed some animation. 'The only local history I'm interested in is *yours*, Andrew. And you've really been too mysterious about certain things. Tell me, when do you and Christine actually plan to set the wedding date?'

'It's Kristin,' Andrew said.

Joanna smiled at him. 'When *is* the wedding date?'

He set down the menu he'd been perusing. 'Now that you've brought it up, I have something to tell both you and your father—'

'Let's go ahead and order,' Kristin said, snapping open her own menu. 'I'm famished. Mr. Larcum, I understand the ratatouille is delicious.'

She didn't know why she was now the one delaying the inevitable. She ignored Andrew's thoughtful glance, and she certainly ignored Joanna's calculating one. Instead, she engaged Mr. Larcum in a detailed discussion of French versus American cookery.

It wasn't until dessert that the conversation lagged again. Kristin stared at the pineapple compote she'd ordered, wishing that this evening was over and done with.

Joanna leaned toward her. 'You and Andrew haven't eaten a whole lot tonight. Perhaps being engaged dampens the appetite.'

Andrew set down his fork without tasting the slice of rum cake in front of him. 'Mr. Larcum,' he said, his expression determined. 'Ben, that is. Kristin and I appreciate this invitation tonight—'

'Joanna and I have wanted the opportunity to know you better,' interrupted Mr. Larcum. 'I can tell you we're much closer to a decision about signing a contract with you.'

'That's good to hear,' Andrew said, still with a look of grim determination. 'But before you make a decision, there's something you should know. Kristin and I . . . the truth is—'

'The truth is,' Kristin burst out, 'Andrew and I are no longer engaged. You see, we've . . . we've broken up! When you invited us to dinner, we didn't know how to tell you.'

Three startled faces confronted her. But no one could have been more startled than Kristin herself. She wasn't used to inventing stories, but she was inventing this one with frightful vividness. Words popped out of her mouth before she could censor them.

'Mr. Larcum, this has been a lovely evening. If Andrew and I have seemed distracted, I do hope you'll understand. This type of thing is so difficult for everyone concerned . . .'

'Yes, yes, of course,' said Mr. Larcum, obviously perturbed. 'I'm very sorry to hear about this, Dr. Mabry—may I call you Kristin? You see, Kristin, I believed you and Andrew made an excellent couple. Joanna

213

agreed with me. Didn't you, my dear?'

'A marvelous couple,' Joanna said, with only the slightest hint of irony. She glanced from Kristin to Andrew. 'It appears you've left your ex-fiancé speechless. Andrew, do say something about this. My father and I are all turned around.'

But Andrew didn't speak. He merely gazed at Kristin, his eyebrows drawn together in a puzzled frown. She gazed back at him, not knowing what to say next herself. What was wrong with her? Instead of helping to clear up this fracas, she'd only made it worse!

Beep-beep-beep. It was Kristin's pager going off, and she'd never been so grateful to hear that sound. 'Excuse me,' she said, scooting back her chair. 'An emergency call. I'll be right back.'

She hurried from the restaurant and out into the hotel lobby. At one of the desk phones she quickly dialled her answering service, and a moment later she was speaking to a flustered pet owner.

'No, Mrs. Meyers, don't worry,' Kristin said soothingly. 'Cats get into fights like this all the time. Bring Blackout to the hospital as soon as you can, and we'll have him stitched up before you know it. Yes, I'll be leaving to meet you there. I'm on my way.'

She hung up the phone; unfortunately, Joanna had followed her out to the lobby and now perched gracefully on the edge of a gilt chair.

'My, Kristin, you've given us such a surprise. And before we've even had a chance to recover, you're leaving.'

'Glad to see you can remember my name when it suits you,' Kristin remarked.

'So I like to have a little fun now and then. No harm intended. But I'm really beginning to wonder about *you*. What's gone wrong between you and Andrew?'

Kristin glanced impatiently at the clock. 'I do have an emergency to take care of, Joanna. If you'll just give my apologies to your father and Andrew—'

'I don't understand you at all. You're in love with Andrew, but you're running away from him. In my mind, that constitutes the *real* emergency.'

Kristin stared at the other woman. 'In love with him ... Of course I'm not in love with him!'

Joanna settled back in her chair, crossing one shapely leg over the other. As usual, she managed to look lovely in spite of her indifferent choice of clothes. 'I used to have my eye on Andrew myself. To be honest, I was even hoping I could break up your engagement. But then ... I could see how the two of you felt about each other. I'm smart. I know when I should move on and leave the field to someone else. Face it, Kristin. You and Andrew are mad about each other. Why this nonsense with splitting up?'

Kristin gave a strangled sort of laugh, her emotions all in a hopeless jumble. The breakup was nonsense, all right, but in a way Joanna Larcum couldn't even begin to imagine. 'Sometimes people simply don't belong together,' Kristin said. 'It's better to find that out before it's too late. Now, I really have to go.'

'You and Andrew *do* belong together. I'm not vice president of personnel for nothing—I see what goes on with people. Of course, if you're going to dump Andrew, maybe he should have someone around who'll console him. I might be just what he needs.' Joanna looked pleased with herself. She stood and began drifting back toward the restaurant. 'Kristin, I do believe you'd better go handle that emergency of yours. Don't worry—I'll take care of Andrew.'

This whole mess was only getting worse and worse! Because now Kristin couldn't bear the thought of Joanna Larcum comforting Andrew over the fake breakup of his fake engagement. She was tempted to march right back into that restaurant and give Joanna some *real* competition...

But instead, with a small moan, Kristin turned and hurried out of the Sequoyah Hotel.

CHAPTER EIGHT

Kristin sat in her office at the animal hospital, making notes on a patient chart. 'Freckles is a terrier cross, age three years, all vaccinations current...' She stifled a weary yawn and set her pen down for a moment. This was only a temporary respite in her schedule. Several more appointments were lined up for the rest of the afternoon, including a large Doberman named Sam who squealed if you so much as pointed a needle in his direction. Kristin wasn't looking forward to Sam, not at all. And she still had to write up her notes for the speech she was giving next week at the community center. Her topic would be the proper spaying and neutering of pets, something she felt very strongly about. Usually Kristin wouldn't have any trouble coming up with the words she needed for this type of speech, but today all she wanted to do was shut her eyes, rest her head on her arms and forget every responsibility.

It wasn't really her schedule that was at fault. No, it was the fact that she hadn't been sleeping well ever since the end of her so-called engagement. And no matter how much she tried to bury herself in her work, Andrew O'Donnell kept intruding into her mind. She couldn't seem to concentrate anymore on being a veterinarian or a mother—or on simply being herself. These days she felt incomplete, unfinished somehow. She was reminded of a melody she'd once heard, a melody that didn't have a satisfactory ending. Even after the music had died away, Kristin had strained to hear the notes left unplayed. That was how her life felt now—as if there were too many notes left unplayed.

A knock came at the office door and she swiveled around in her chair. 'Come in,' she called.

The door swung open to reveal Andrew. She looked at him warily.

'Hello,' she said.

'Hi. I'm here to pick up Randy.'

They'd been polite to each other the past few days—too polite. They hadn't really talked, exchanging only brief greetings whenever Andrew came by for Randy. Now Kristin rushed to fill the silence.

'Randy'll be out in just a minute. He's back in the kennel, visiting one of our newest patients. A chipmunk with a broken leg, if you can believe it. Someone found the poor little creature by the side of the road. I've never set a splint that small before ...' Kristin made a restless gesture. 'Andrew, have a seat, will you? Enough of this. I've been wanting to clear up a few things between us.'

'So have I, as a matter of fact.' He turned his chair around so he could straddle the seat and prop his arms on the back. 'I've been trying to figure out why you wouldn't let me tell the Larcums the truth. Now they not only think our engagement was real, they think our breakup is real, too. We only got ourselves in deeper.'

'I don't know why I did it,' Kristin said with a sigh. 'Maybe I was just trying to do you a favor. After all, Mr. Larcum will be a lot more kindly disposed toward you if he doesn't feel deceived.'

'Right now Ben Larcum only thinks I'm crazy. He can't understand why I'd let a woman like you get away.'

Kristin pulled another animal's chart in front of her and studied it intently. 'Joanna implied almost the same thing to me—why was I letting a man like you get away. We really convinced the two of them, Andrew. Joanna thinks we're actually in love. What a joke we've managed to play on ourselves.'

'Is it a joke?' he asked quietly.

She gazed at him. 'You tell me.' Her voice was unsteady.

Andrew didn't say anything for a long while. When at last he did speak, he sounded brusque. 'Hell, I don't know anything anymore, Kristin. You've been pushing me away the entire time you've known me. You still don't trust me.'

Kristin slapped down the chart. 'Why should I trust you? I don't even know how you feel about me.'

'None of this was supposed to happen,'

Andrew muttered as if to himself. 'I was just looking for a breather, a little time-out from women. Was that so much to want?'

Kristin had practically asked Andrew flat out how he felt about her, and all he could say was that he needed a breather. She felt like she'd walked up to a swimming pool and poked a toe in the water—only to find out that it was freezing cold.

She dug into one of the pockets of her lab coat and brought out a folded handkerchief. She unfolded it to reveal the diamond ring nestled inside.

'I've been meaning to give this back to you,' she said in a crisp voice. 'It won't matter anymore if you return it to Larcum. Any way you look at it, the engagement is over. We can both get on with our lives.'

He gave her a dissatisfied glance. 'We still have to hash this out.'

'You've already made yourself perfectly clear, Andrew. Look, maybe we both got a little confused, a little too caught up in the roles we were playing. But now we aren't playing those roles any longer. The engagement is over!'

He seemed about to say more when Randy came bursting into the office. Andrew silently pocketed the ring and turned his attention to Randy. A few moments later, Kristin stood at the window and watched the two of them leave for another visit to the video arcade: a boy who

220

needed a father, a man so good with her son. She blinked at the sudden tears that blurred her vision, tears that shimmered in the Oklahoma sunlight.

Why was she making a fool of herself and starting to sniffle? Joanna Larcum, of course, wanted to blame it all on love. And Kristin began to wonder if perhaps Joanna was right, after all.

The possibility had to be faced, no matter how distressing. Could it be that Kristin had actually gone and fallen in love with Andrew O'Donnell?

*   *   *

Rich, moist soil. A garden trowel and a packet of forget-me-not seeds. It should have been an irresistible combination, guaranteed to soothe Kristin's frazzled nerves. Instead, her nerves were simply fraying all the more. She knelt in the damp soil, wielding her trowel distractedly. What was wrong with her? Why couldn't she simply push Andrew out of her mind? For two whole weeks, she'd done such a good job of avoiding him. Whenever he came to the house or the hospital to pick up Randy, she made certain she was in another room—unavailable. After fourteen long days of not allowing herself even a glimpse of Andrew, she ought to be able to concentrate on something else. But here she was, still stewing about him.

She threw down her trowel in disgust and climbed the porch steps. Plunking herself down in one of the creaky wicker chairs, she took a sip of iced tea. Then she pressed the cool glass against her forehead, seeking some relief from the heat. Holmes was stretched out on the porch railing, his calico coat glossy in the sun. Sherlock dozed at Kristin's feet, too sleepy to chase cats today. Kristin wished fervently that she could emulate the relaxed attitude of her animals.

A red Bronco pulled into the drive, and a moment later Andrew came striding up the walk, fresh and vibrant. He wore black jeans and cowboy boots, his denim shirt a pleasing faded blue. With his charcoal hair and dark gray eyes, he was easily the most handsome man in Danfield—the most handsome man in Oklahoma, for that matter. Kristin glared at him.

'What are you doing here?' she asked. 'You're not supposed to pick up Randy this afternoon. He's off playing with his friend Jonah.'

Andrew ignored her. He stopped at the bottom of the porch steps and solemnly addressed the cat. 'Holmes, seems Kristin and I have a problem,' he said. 'We're looking to you for advice.'

Holmes blinked slowly, wisely, at Andrew. Now Kristin glared at both of them. With a defiant air, she reached into her glass of tea and fished out an ice cube. She popped it down the front of her T-shirt. Andrew glanced at her, then back at Holmes. 'That's still damn distracting,' he confided in the cat. He came up a step and rested his elbow on the porch railing.

Showing no compunction at all, Kristin popped another ice cube down her shirt. 'What do you want, Andrew?'

He gave Holmes a gentle rub on the head. Holmes closed his eyes in feline contentment. And then Andrew smiled at Kristin. 'I thought you might be interested to know that Ben Larcum signed a contract with me last week. He's agreed to carry O'Donnell timepieces in every one of his department stores.'

Kristin forgot that she was trying to be angry. 'Oh, I'm thrilled for you,' she said. 'Really thrilled. You worked so hard to get that contract, and now O'Donnell's Fine Timepieces can be everything you've planned.'

'You should know something else.' Andrew came up another step and leaned down to pet Sherlock. The dog wagged his tail happily, and Andrew went on. 'Before Mr. Larcum signed, I told him the truth about you and me. I told him the engagement was bogus from the beginning.'

'I see.' Kristin set her glass on the table. 'He knew the truth, yet he went ahead and signed a contract with you? Wasn't he upset in the least?'

Now Andrew's smile was rueful. 'It turns

out that Ben Larcum has a surprisingly good sense of humor. He chuckled for the damnedest long while, and then he advised me to get myself engaged for real this time.'

Kristin listened to the pounding of her own heart and tried to be nonchalant. 'I'm sure Joanna Larcum's more than willing to be your fiancée. Why don't you give her a whirl?'

Andrew moved toward Kristin. 'Afraid Joanna isn't my type. No ... you're the one elected for the job, Dr. Mabry.'

She struggled to her feet, almost tripping over Sherlock in her agitation. 'What are you talking about? I can't tolerate any more of this pretend—'

'I'm talking about the real thing this time. I'm offering you a bona fide, authentic and completely genuine husband. Namely myself.' He gave her another of his slow, easy grins and came closer.

She took a step back. She couldn't believe what she was hearing. She *wouldn't* believe it. This was too much like all her secret dreams of the past few weeks. 'Forget it, Andrew. No how, no way. Why should I believe that you want to marry me? I mean, first, all you can say is that you need a breather, and then—'

'Took me a while to figure out, that's all.' He advanced toward her purposefully. 'Telling the whole story to Mr. Larcum was a real eye opener. It made me see that what I needed was right in front of me. It's you, Kristin. You're what's been right in front of me. A ready-made fiancée.'

She backed away from him again, but she was starting to run out of porch. 'If you want a fiancée, go find somebody else for the job.' By now she was pressed right against the wooden railing, but Andrew still wouldn't give up. He took another step closer.

'No one else will do for this particular job,' he said matter-of-factly. 'Believe me, I've had enough trouble with women to know what I'm talking about. I'll tell you what the problem was all along, Dr. Mabry. I just hadn't found the right woman yet. I needed a woman with gold hair, a son named Randy, a cat who gives advice and enough other animals to fill a zoo.'

Kristin was finding it hard to breathe evenly. 'Please stop, Andrew.'

He gazed at her, his expression intent. 'I came back to Danfield because I was missing something in my life, Kristin, something very important.' His voice grew husky. 'I thought it would be enough to revive my family business. I thought that was all I'd been missing. I wouldn't listen when the honorable judge told me I needed a family, not just a family business. But then I met you and Randy, and somehow forty hours started to seem like a very short time. I took on another forty hours, but even that doesn't seem like it'll be enough. I'm starting to think more in terms of forty years.'

It took all of Kristin's willpower not to fold

herself into his arms that very minute. But she was still afraid. 'Andrew,' she whispered. 'I don't know if I can trust again.'

'I'm not your ex-husband,' he said firmly. 'Maybe it takes me a while to figure out that the woman I need is standing right in front of me, but once I do, I'm smart enough not to let her go. You'll learn to trust me, Kristin. You'll have those forty years or more to learn.'

He took a ring box out of his pocket and opened it with a flourish. A second later he slipped the small, familiar diamond onto Kristin's finger. 'Still fits,' he observed. 'How about it, Dr. Mabry? Will you marry me?'

'No,' she said, even as she wiggled her finger and watched the diamond sparkle in the sun. 'No, I won't marry you, Andrew O'Donnell.'

'Give me three good reasons why not.'

He was standing so close to her that her toes nudged the tips of his cowboy boots. She took a deep breath, but that didn't help her think any more clearly.

'Three reasons,' she muttered. 'That's easy. First off, I told myself I was never going to get married again—that I was never going to make another mistake like that. And the second reason ...' She tried to think of all the old excuses, but nothing came to mind. For so long she'd used those excuses to protect herself, holding them to her like a shabby coat that would somehow keep her warm. But at the moment she didn't seem to need any extra

226

warmth. The sun was shining down on her, thick and pure as honey, and Andrew brought his arms around her. Now his expression was grave, but she could've sworn he was quietly laughing.

'It wouldn't be a mistake to marry me, Kristin. You know that, but you just won't admit it.'

'All right, give me three good reasons why I *should* marry you!'

'That's easy. First off, I love you, Kristin. And the other two reasons—'

'Can't think of any, can you?' She was trembling in his arms, her hands spread against his chest.

'Reasons two and three—I love you, Kristin. And I love you. I can come up with as many of those reasons as you like.'

She gazed at him, still not daring to believe. She made one last struggle to hold on to her old excuses against love, but they fell away from her like the tattered fears they were. In Andrew's arms, she began to realize she couldn't stay afraid much longer.

'Oh, Andrew … I didn't plan on you. I didn't plan on your making me hope again.'

'I want you to hope like it's the first time.' His voice was suddenly fierce. 'The first time for both of us. We're starting something new here.'

'Brand-new.' And that was exactly how she felt right now, as new and joyful as someone on the brink of love for the very first time. Andrew was showing her that her future could be so much different than the past. When she'd moved to Oklahoma and found him, she'd done a whole lot more than cross a state line. She'd crossed into the unexplored territory of her own heart.

'I suppose it *is* pretty convenient,' she said at last. 'I mean, we already have the engagement ring.'

'The way I look at it, we've already done the engagement,' he pointed out. 'What do you say we get married right away?'

She nodded, filled with a peaceful, sure happiness. 'I know one little boy who'd be awfully glad about that.'

'Think he'll let us sneak off on a honeymoon?'

'Anything to have a real dad at last. Andrew ... are you ever going to kiss me?'

It was actually several kisses later that Kristin broke away from her fiancé—her bona fide, genuine, authentic fiancé. 'I seem to have forgotten one detail,' she said rather breathlessly.

'Mmm. What's that?' Andrew brushed his lips over her cheek, obviously getting ready for another serious kiss. Which was fine with Kristin, but there was still that one small detail.

'Andrew, I almost forgot to tell you. The fact of the matter is ... I love you, too. Quite a lot.'

Before Andrew even had a chance to answer,

a tousled blond head poked up above the porch railing, and Randy gazed with obvious satisfaction at his mother and his future dad. Clambering up onto the railing, he didn't seem surprised in the least to find the two adults locked in an embrace.

'Mom, when's the wedding gonna be?' Randy asked seriously. 'Jonah says I have to wear a suit. Does Andrew have to wear a suit?'

Kristin and Andrew laughed at the same time, but it was Andrew who spoke. 'Son, you and I are going to wear the finest tuxedos around. We're going to celebrate our wedding like nothing you've ever seen. But for now...'

For now, Andrew kissed Kristin. For now, and forever.